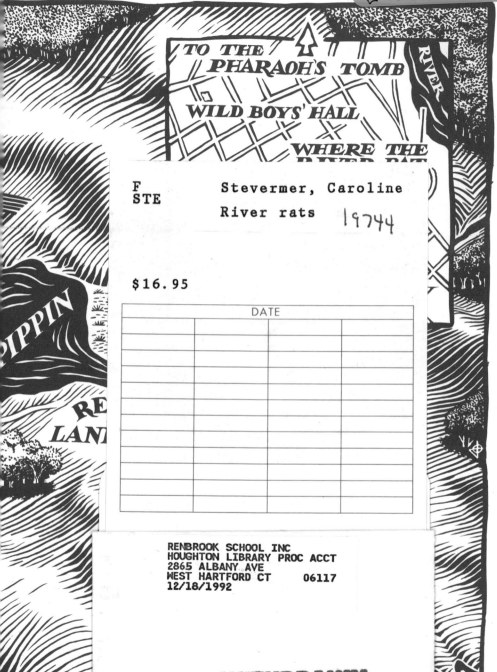

P9-DMV-218

TO THE
PHARAOH'S TOMB

RIVER

WILD BOYS' HALL

WHERE THE
RIVER RAT

PIPPIN

RE
LAN

F
STE

Stevermer, Caroline

River rats   19744

$16.95

DATE			

River Rats

RIVER

JANE YOLEN BOOKS

HARCOURT BRACE JOVANOVICH, PUBLISHERS

San Diego   New York   London

CAROLINE STEVERMER

RATS

Copyright © 1992 by Caroline Stevermer

Library of Congress Cataloging-in-Publication Data
Stevermer, Caroline.
River rats/Caroline Stevermer. — 1st ed.
p.   cm.
"Jane Yolen books."
Summary: Nearly twenty years after the holocaust called the Flash
has destroyed modern civilization, Tomcat and a group of other orphans
face danger as they steer an old steamboat over the toxic waters
of the Mississippi River.
ISBN 0-15-200895-0
[1. Science fiction.   2. Mississippi River — Fiction.]   I. Title.
PZ7.S84856Ri   1992
[Fic] — dc20   91-58578

Designed by Trina Stahl
Printed in the United States of America
First edition   A B C D E

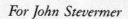

For John Stevermer

ACKNOWLEDGMENT

This book began because of Terri Windling, creator of the River Rat Revue. Compared with other fires she's kindled, this is a small spark, but it has burned stubbornly for years. May she find the result worth the wait.

CONTENTS

PROLOGUE

THE ONLY TROUBLE WITH THE RIVER IS you can't drink it. You can float on it with a raft or a canoe. Or a paddle wheel steamboat. Or you can swim in it, if you absolutely have to. But if you try to swim, better keep your mouth shut. If you swallow any water, you're in for a rough time afterward. River water looks brown and greasy, like real bad gravy only thinner. It's toxic. If you drink it, you die. Sure, everybody dies sometime. But there are better ways.

A paddle wheel steamboat pumps the river water up, boils it, and uses the steam for power. Heading upstream, a steamboat makes a steady seven miles an hour. Better than a raft, which can't go upstream at all. Faster than a canoe, and not quite such hard work. For more than a hundred years before the Flash and almost twenty years since, there were no paddle wheelers on the river. But we have one. We have the River Rat.

It's hard for me to describe the River Rat. How do you describe home? To me she doesn't look like anything but herself. When I look at her, I don't see her red paddle wheel, or her three decks, once painted gray but now flaked down almost to bare wood. I don't see

I

yards of deck rail like wooden lace. I do notice the pair of black smokestacks, but not as much for their height or fancy crowns as for the steady billow of smoke they put out. Anyway, it isn't so much what you see of the River Rat *as what you feel on board — the pounding of the paddle wheel, the vibration of the decks when you're under way — that tells you best what she is.*

Back before the Flash, the River Rat *was a museum. She was made according to the old designs. She must have cost somebody a lot of money, because once she was as nice inside as she is outside. The way they built her, she could have traveled up and down the river as easy as an otter crosses a stream. Instead, they kept her like a dog on a leash. She was tied up in a marina to educate people about the history of the river. After the Flash, when everything changed, the* River Rat *became an orphanage school.*

Nobody knows for sure what happened during the Flash. Everybody thinks they know, just like they think they know about everything else that ever happened. But the truth is, nobody really knows anything — which tells you how bad it was. Bombs or gas or germ warfare . . . it must have been something.

For fifteen years after the Flash, hundreds of kids came and went at the marina. They were clothed and fed and taught to read and write and figure. As far back as I can remember, I was at that school. I hardly noticed that where I lived was any different from the other buildings near the marina. I learned to read and write and always to boil water before I drank it. That seemed like plenty of schooling to me.

I was ten when Toby and Esteban came to the orphanage. They were three or four years older than me. They'd had some education somewhere before they came and were old enough to look after themselves. They were at the school for learning, not just for meals.

But somehow Toby and Esteban didn't fit in very well at the school. The teachers did the best they could. But Toby could never be satisfied with what the teachers told us out of books. She had to question everything. Esteban didn't stop there. He had to read the books himself and question every adult who would listen. The teachers had a lot to do, and they didn't like to be questioned. Pretty soon they left Toby and Esteban out of regular classes to learn on their own.

It was Esteban and Toby who found the museum records and showed us kids what the River Rat *had once been. They taught us what she could be again if we cared enough to learn. They found books about life on the river and taught us about soundings and fathoms.*

I was eleven when we set the River Rat *free. We didn't steal her. We saved her. There was a big storm coming in and the orphans were supposed to be taken away to higher ground. But the cart never came back for the last dozen kids. It was hot. The sky turned green and bruised-looking. The air was so wet and warm, it got hard to breathe. Then the wind began to rise.*

After a little of that wind, we knew the storm was going to be the worst we'd ever seen. It wasn't safe for us to stay. The River Rat *would be smashed into kindling against the mooring. It wasn't even safe for us to leave. Every wharf in the marina was bucking like a pony. Yet we had to go.*

The younger kids helped me break up desks and chairs and tables. Toby used the wood from the broken furniture to start a fire in the River Rat's *firebox. Esteban ran the pump that filled the boilers with river water. Soon the* River Rat *had plumes of smoke coming out of her stacks. A head of steam woke her engines from their long sleep. The kids helped me cast off the mooring line. Esteban set a course for open water.*

3

You can't learn everything out of books. We had a rough ride. A dozen times we came close to disaster. Somehow Toby kept the boilers from blowing up. The kids and I kept the Rat *clear of snags and shallow water. Esteban steered us to safety.*

We were at a landing forty miles upriver when the gale blew in. Maybe it wasn't too safe to stay aboard her during severe weather, but that far upriver the storm wasn't much more than hard rain. And we didn't feel right about leaving the boat alone after she got us away. The River Rat *saved us. The least we could do was stay aboard and look out for her.*

In a few days we returned to the marina and put ashore the kids who wanted to go home. But by the time the storm had blown itself inside out, Esteban, Toby, and I knew we were already home, free on the river with the Rat.

It didn't take us long to discover that if we took care of her and kept her running—on scrounged coal and bartered firewood and smashed furniture—the Rat *would take care of us. Since then, Lindy and Spike and Jake have joined our crew. Together we run the* River Rat. *Mostly we trade music, news, and mail for drinking water, food, and clothing. We haul some cargo. We never carry passengers.*

I've seen the pictures in old books. There used to be a lot of ways to travel around: planes and trains and cars and boats and bikes and blimps. I've never had a chance to try those other ways, but just by looking I can tell you that a paddle wheel steamboat has them all beat. It's like living in a house that moves, yet it sometimes seems to be the one thing in the world that holds still. You feel the deck alive beneath you while the river unwinds all around you. It's life, that's what: the only life for me.

I

ON BOARD

E WERE NORTHBOUND IN THE UP-per river, just above Dresbach, where the deepest part of the channel draws in to the western shore. Esteban had us so close to the riverbank that poplar leaves drifted down and stuck to the deck like yellow paper hearts. It was late in the year to be on the upper river, one of those clear autumn days when the sun shines so bright that everything in the world has a fine black line around it.

As the *River Rat* came up the channel, I was in my usual place, at the bow with the sounding pole, waiting for Esteban to call for the depth. Lindy was admiring the scenery from the rail of the upper deck.

Scenery is easier to admire from up there than from the main deck. Where I stood, about all I could see of shore was a tangle of briars and silvery poplar trunks. Here and there big old willows were hanging out over the water like they were trying to judge the drop before they fell in. The current washes the shore right out from under them until only their roots hold the trunk up. One day the roots go, the tree falls, and the river has a new snag all ready to rip the hull out of the next steamboat that gets too close. It's hard to enjoy that sort of scenery from the bow when the *Rat* is so close to shore that leaves are landing on the deck.

But then, I wasn't supposed to be looking at the scenery. I was supposed to be looking at the river and leaning on the pole.

When Esteban called for soundings, Lindy would relay the order to me. All I had to do was keep my eyes on the water and listen for Lindy. But what I heard instead was shouting and hounds barking. I peered ashore to see where the noise was coming from. Except for briars and poplars and next year's snags, which were all sliding past me at seven miles an hour, I couldn't see a thing.

I turned to look up at Lindy. "Can you see anything?" I called.

Lindy was leaning over the rail, watching something intently. "Not yet," she called back. "But whatever it is, it's headed this way."

I listened hard. There's something in the sound of a hound hunting — more a hoot than a bark — that's hard to mistake. The hounds I heard were hunting. The shouting wasn't so clear. I was trying to make out the words when Lindy stiffened and leaned far out on the rail, pointing. "There!" she called.

I followed the line of her dark green sleeve and caught a glimpse of gray and brown moving through the sway of branches ashore.

"Hey, mister," Lindy shouted. "Mister! Look out. You're too close to the edge."

I saw him then: fifty, maybe a hundred yards ahead of us, an old guy in a gray overcoat, his muddy-colored hair straggling in rattails on his shoulders. He looked scared, even under the grime and stubble on his face. He was running toward us along the bank, beating branches out of his way with desperate haste. He was so close to the water's edge that the dirt his boots dislodged fell into the river.

Behind him the cry of the hunting hounds was coming closer.

Up in the pilothouse, Esteban must have seen him, too. I heard the muffled chime of his signal to Spike in the engine room. The *River Rat's* speed began to slacken.

There was a firm boot tread behind me, and Jake joined me at the rail, life preserver and rope in his hands. From overhead came Toby's calm voice: "Soundings, Tomcat."

I got busy. I never mind the first sounding. Nice dry pole, smooth reach over the rail to plunge it down into the oily river. Easy. It's the second sounding, when the pole comes up all slimy, that I hate. And the third, and the thirtieth, when my shoulders are aching and my spine feels like it's going to crack. Soundings wear me out.

"Mark three," I called over my shoulder as I brought the pole back up. It was hard to ignore the commotion and pay attention to the markings on my sounding pole, but orders are orders. Especially Toby's. The way I learned it, mark three is three fathoms, eighteen feet of water. The *Rat* draws nine. Feet, not fathoms.

"They've got him," Lindy said.

I looked up from the second sounding. There was a yellow dog at the old guy's elbow, snapping at the sleeve of his ragged coat. Men were coming out of the tangled underbrush now, big men. Some of them carried clubs. The old guy was still trying to

7

scramble along the riverbank, but the dog would probably have him down in a minute. I put my eyes back on the river and kept them there. I didn't want to see. Anyway, Toby was waiting for the next sounding.

"By the mark three," I called. I plunged the pole down again. "Quarter twain." That's thirteen and a half feet. Not quite the comfortable fit we'd had before. I hoped Esteban had his eyes on the channel, not on the old guy.

There was a big splash from the riverbank and a roar from the men on shore. I kept my attention on the soundings. Another splash, a small one — Jake had thrown the life preserver. I snatched a quick look. The men on shore were roaring at us. About time they noticed we were there.

I felt the change in our course through the deck as Esteban steered toward shore. Then I saw it in the sounding. "Mark twain," I called. Only twelve feet now. Three to spare.

I stole another look over my shoulder as I sent the pole down again. Toby was still on the upper deck rail. Lindy had come down to stand at the rail beside Jake and was hauling on the life preserver line with him. I couldn't see the old guy, but I heard splashing. The men on shore were so close I could see their faces, red with sunburn or anger or both. "Quarter less twain!" I called. My voice squeaked a little. Ten and a half feet. Eighteen inches to spare.

Somebody on shore threw something, and the splash hit me as I came up from the next sounding. I spat and called, "Ten feet."

"Esteban." Toby's voice, usually soft, can carry when she wants it to. "Tomcat says ten feet."

8

"Nine and a half," I told her. I was glad my voice sounded as calm as hers.

Beneath my feet the deck seemed to shift somehow. Esteban was drawing us away from the western bank. I could only spare a glimpse back. Out of the corner of my eye I saw Jake and Lindy haul the life preserver in over the rail. It looked like there was a big bundle of gray rags with it.

"Ten feet," I called.

The *River Rat* picked up speed. The men and hounds ashore were trying to keep pace with us. They'd get sick of that soon enough. I kept up the soundings. "Mark twain. Quarter twain. Mark three. By the mark three."

I slid a look along the rail as we reached the safer depth of mark three. Jake and Lindy were working over the old guy. It was like twisting a mop. River water was coming off him by the bucketful. Little streams were running across the deck in every direction.

The men on shore were well behind us and still shouting. I didn't catch anything special in their words, but I leaned over the rail and made a gesture back.

Toby's voice came down from the upper deck like a bucket of snow. "Soundings, Tomcat."

When we're under way, Toby can't give orders to Esteban, but she can make the rest of us move any time she wants to. I went back to my soundings.

The *River Rat*'s paddle wheel took us upstream at a steady eighteen beats a minute. Esteban, with his usual sense of space and time, had brought us safely through the trough of current close to shore. We were back in the broad depths at the heart of the river. When I took the twentieth sounding, my pole struck nothing. I drew back with a deep sigh and let the pole rest on the deck. "No bottom," I called up to Toby. "No bottom at all."

Toby touched the brim of her hat to me, a sketchy salute. I grinned back and started to stretch the ache out of my arms.

The old guy seemed to be trying to struggle away from Jake and Lindy. He was weak and couldn't do much, since they had him rolled in a blanket. They knelt on the deck, working to save him from the river. Jake held his head so Lindy could spoon cooking oil down his throat. It worked great. The old guy brought up all the river water he'd swallowed. As he vomited, Jake drew back in disgust. The mess on the deck was getting profound.

"He's so cold. We're going to need another blanket," said Lindy. Her hands were dirty, so she had to push her hair out of her eyes with the back of her wrist. The knees of her gray pants were soaked and there were dark stains on the front of her green shirt. She didn't seem to care, or to notice the mess on the deck. It takes a lot to disgust Lindy.

When Jake came back with the extra blanket, Toby was with him. She had her hands shoved deep into the pockets of her overcoat. She does that when she's worried. I think it's so you don't see that she's clenched her fists until the knuckles show white.

"Well?" said Toby. She studied Lindy and the old guy. "What have you got?"

Lindy looked up, green eyes bright beneath the crest of hair that dropped down over her forehead. She brushed it away with the back of her wrist and smiled. "He's alive," she said. "He's empty." She held the old guy's head in her lap. His long hair straggled across her other wrist like rotten string.

Jake shook his head as he brushed at the front of his blue jacket. "I should hope so."

Toby's dark eyes narrowed. "You hauled him out. What are you going to do with him?"

Jake and Lindy exchanged startled looks. Lindy studied the old guy. He seemed to have fallen asleep. The bones of his face were easy to see under the dirt and stubble. He had a lot of cheekbone and nose, not as much jaw. The corners of his wide mouth were pulled down in a grimace. He didn't exactly look like deckhand material. Wrapped up so snug in the blankets, he looked more like a cigar.

"When he wakes up," said Lindy, "we'll find out what he's good at."

Jake shook his head. "First ask him who was chasing him and why."

Lindy paid no attention. "He must be stronger than he looks. He's good at running," she continued, "and he's not a bad swimmer. He jumped in and struck out for us like an expert."

"He wasn't swimming toward us," Jake replied. "He was running away from them. You saw him when he jumped. From the look on his face, he didn't care if he sank or not. He only wanted to get away."

"Do what you want," said Toby, "but remember — no passengers."

Lindy looked at Jake. "If you help me get him to a cabin, we can dry him off and feed him as soon as he wakes up. Then he can tell us why those guys were after him."

"And then he can tell you how he's going to work for his passage to the next landing," said Toby.

Lindy nodded firmly. "Right. I was just going to say that." She picked up the old guy's shoulders. "Do you think you can manage his feet?"

Jake got a grip on them and helped her hoist.

I watched them go, wondering how long it would take Lindy to cook up some feeble chore for the old guy to do while we hauled him upriver. The more useless he turned out to be, the more likely it was that Lindy would find a way keep him safely under her wing.

Something, maybe my expression, annoyed Toby. "You're not a passenger here either, you know," she said. With her black hair, her dark hat and coat, and her head tilted to one side, she looked a little like some kind of black bird. "Get busy and scrub this deck."

Together we mopped up the deck, replaced the life preserver, and coiled the wet line. I kept quiet while we worked. I can't always tell what Toby is thinking just by looking at her. But when she moves quick and fierce, the way she did with that mop, it's not hard to guess. She worries. Just because she's our captain doesn't mean she's responsible for the *River Rat* and everyone aboard. But don't tell her *I* said so.

Toby wears a top hat. The lining of her coat hangs in taffeta tatters out of the cuffs, so every gesture she makes is a little larger than anyone else's. She wears boots like Jake's, high and heavy-soled, but there's no way to mistake her step, quick and quiet, for Jake's tread. Lindy says Toby wears a top hat so she'll look taller. If that's so, it doesn't work. There's no hiding the fact she's nearly the shortest of the River Rats. She's smaller than any of us except Spike, who doesn't really count, because he's youngest. Anyway, judging by the size of his feet, he won't be the shortest for long.

When she was satisfied with the deck, Toby handed me the mop and went almost silently up the stair, headed to the top deck and the pilothouse. Esteban would be expecting a report on the arrival of our guest.

When Toby was gone, I leaned on the mop and looked out across the river at the western shore. I looked and I listened. It wasn't possible, of course, because we were headed upstream at seven miles an hour, but I could almost fool myself into thinking I could hear hounds hunting off in the distance. I closed my eyes to listen better. This time it didn't work.

There was the steady thrash of the paddle wheel, one of the most familiar sounds of the *River Rat*. Lindy's voice lifted enough to drift down to me from the upper deck, not words, just tone of voice — surprise tinged with disgust, I judged. She must be helping Jake undress the old guy. I put the mop away and went to the engine room to tell Spike he'd missed all the excitement.

We're lucky Spike joined us aboard the *River Rat*. But Spike is just as lucky we joined him. We found him working a shunting engine in a rail yard south of Saint Loo. We were ashore mining an abandoned coal car for fuel. When we met him, he had a chain around one ankle. The people who made him run the engine thought he might forget how nice they were and go away. Spike wouldn't say a word — not to them, not to us, not to anybody. He needed help bad. We did what we could. First we filed through the chain. Then we fixed the people who put it on him so they couldn't bother anybody else. Ever.

After that it seemed like a good idea to take Spike home with us to the *River Rat*. That trip wasn't much fun. To begin with, we didn't have enough food with us. Spike could have eaten every crumb we had and still looked pitiful. Just looked, mind. He still wasn't saying a word. On top of that, even with the shunting engine to help, we had a *lot* of coal to haul.

When we finally got back to our landing, Spike's blue eyes went wide, and he started talking about water levels and flame beds. Our eyes went wide and we realized it wasn't just a good idea. It was a brilliant idea. Spike has never quit talking since. He stepped into the *River Rat*'s engine room the way I step into my jeans.

He loves those engines. When he's with them, he smiles all the time. Otherwise he just looks like any kid, with maybe more than his share of feet and knees and elbows. He's real pale, so against his skin his hair seems unnaturally red. The spikes look unnatural, too, but only until you see him run his fingers through his hair. Then you understand how he got his name.

If he's alone, if the engines are running smooth, and if there's nothing to do but put the occasional shovelful of coal into the firebox, Spike practices drumming. Sometimes he uses drumsticks. More often he uses whatever comes to hand. One night he got started with two lug wrenches on an empty pipe. The noise went all over the *Rat*. It sounded like the boiler had fallen out and was scraping along the river bottom. Spike said the engines inspired him.

When I got to the engine room, Spike was stoking. He put a few pounds of coal into the red glow of embers already in the firebox, closed the door, and leaned on his shovel. "Well? What did I miss this time?"

"Everything," I replied. I stretched and yawned and took my favorite seat, an upturned bucket. "A guy tried to race us with no boat."

"That's not what Jake said." Spike put the shovel back in its corner. "He came down to see if I needed any help shoveling coal."

"There's an idea," I said. "Passengers are bad luck, and he's got to work his way. So we'll put him to work shoveling coal. He can use a spoon. I don't think he can lift anything heavier."

"Maybe he can cook," Spike suggested.

"Hey, *I* cook."

"You call it cooking?" Spike grinned and shook his head. "Ask Esteban when we're going to put in, will you? I want to know if I'll have time to rake out the grates after we make a landing."

"Ask him yourself," I said. "I'll watch things here while you're gone."

Spike shook his head again. "You go, Tomcat. If I go up there, I'll have to listen to him talk about training and instinct, because he thinks I didn't back off the speed fast enough when he rang down here. You go."

I went. I never mind a trip up to the pilothouse.

To watch the river from the pilothouse is like floating. It's like dreaming. It's the best place to be. Picture a room made out of windows set at the very top of the *River Rat*. The view from the windows is always changing, slow but constant. The change is almost the only way you know you're moving, the *River Rat* travels so smooth and steady.

When I got to the pilothouse, three things were there besides the view: a bench at the back, where visitors sit so they don't

15

get in the way, a polished wooden wheel taller than I am, and Esteban.

Esteban is not tall, but he is a big guy. His shoulders are wide, and when he moves you can tell that a lot of muscles are involved. He's dark with dark eyes, same as me and Toby. But there's something about the way Esteban looks at you, so clear and sharp, that makes his eyes seem almost golden. It's like he's catching some kind of light that no one else can see. He knows yoga and t'ai chi and about two hundred other disciplines. I've asked him to teach me, but he never does. Instead he says things like "Breath is the greatest strength" and "Physical strength must be the handservant of spiritual strength." Which may be true, but what does it mean?

Esteban was in his usual place, at the wheel. His hands were light on the spokes, his eyes were on the river ahead, and his attention was on Toby. When Esteban is still, he is perfectly still. From where I stopped at the door, I could see the red jewel he wears in his ear catch the sun and hold it steady.

Toby was pacing — three steps starboard, three steps port. She had her hands jammed far down in her pockets as she moved back and forth. The minute she saw me, she sat down on the bench, suddenly concerned about the sole of her boot. That will teach me to hurry. If I had come up more softly, I might have caught part of their conversation before they knew I was there.

"Spike wants to know when we're going to put in," I said.

Esteban glanced at me, then returned his steady gaze to the river. "Tonight the moon will be nearly full. We can make Red's Landing if it stays clear."

Toby shook her head. "We drop mail off at Fountains."

"Too close to those hunters," Esteban replied.

1 6

"Fountains is on the east bank," said Toby. "The old guy came from the west. And we always get a decent crowd in Fountains. And they've got good water there." Toby sounded like she was trying to convince herself.

"We have water enough for the moment," said Esteban. "It's too close to Dresbach. The *River Rat* is not the only craft that floats."

"It's the fastest thing on this river," Toby said. "Do you think those guys are paddling along after us in dugout canoes?"

"Can you be sure they aren't?" Esteban countered. "Let caution be our guide. Don't linger in Fountains."

"And running all the way to Red's Landing in the dark is your idea of caution," said Toby. She shook her head. "All right. We put in at Fountains. We drop the mail. We stay just long enough to top up the water tanks. And then we head for Red's Landing."

"Tell Spike not to make any plans for this evening," Esteban told me, his grin very white and even in his square face.

Esteban must have rung for more speed while I was on my way down with the message, because when I got to the engine room Spike was stoking again. I gave him the gist of the conversation and waited while he ran his hands through his hair twice thinking about it.

"I'm going to take a nap," he said finally. "It'll help me read Esteban's mind when he's got us dodging snags in the dark."

The rest of the afternoon was pretty dull. I shoveled some coal. I poked around a little. I watched the pressure gauge. There's a red line on it. If the needle crosses the red line, the boiler will explode. The needle didn't move. Esteban didn't ring once. When Spike returned, rubbing his eyes, the bell chimed.

17

"We're there, huh?" I said, reaching for the nearest lever.

Spike caught my wrist and took the lever himself. "He rang early because he thinks you're alone down here and probably won't find the right lever for another few seconds. Wait until he rings again."

"Sure, let him think I'm an idiot," I agreed. "Why not?"

Spike grinned at me. "Where do these rumors get started?"

Esteban rang again. Spike eased back on the lever. The steady slide of the engine slackened. Spike pulled another lever. With a great rush of steam the engine beams slid to a stop. For a moment the deck beneath us lost the vibration that gave it life. The beat of the paddle wheel halted. The silence was eerie. Then Esteban rang for full reverse. Spike hit his switches, and the living racket of the *Rat*'s engines resumed. The deck's familiar steady vibration returned. I let out a breath I hadn't meant to hold. With Spike's hands on the switches in the engine room, and Esteban's hands on the great wheel in the pilothouse, the *River Rat* slid in to Fountains.

2

A WALK IN
THE WOODS

AFTER THE FLASH NOT EVERY TOWN HAD
the pestilence. Not every town had riots and fires and
destruction. There are good places, towns worth a
visit, towns that still work, strung all along the river like beads on
a string.

Some places are big. There are three good cities left. There's
New Orleans, which I would like best even if it wasn't the *Rat*'s
home port. There's Memphis, which I try to give a wide berth,
since they have an orphanage school too and you never know.
And there's Saint Loo, if you like ribs. I wouldn't like to say
anything bad about Saint Loo. Jake might take it wrong. That's
where he came aboard. But the big places need lots of rules to
take care of all their people. Rules don't always agree with us, so
we try to avoid the cities.

Some places are small. It's easier for the small places to be
good, given fertile soil and a safe source of water. You don't have
to have so many rules when you know everybody. There's Dresbach, where the best apples are. There's Thebes, where you can
get the best bread I've ever tasted.

And some places are so small that you can't imagine why anybody ever built anything there at all, except maybe to gaze longingly across the river to the other side. But sometimes those are the best places, where there's nothing to fight over, where you can forget about how tough you are for a few minutes.

Fountains is one of the small places. It is one of the good places. Both good and bad places, regardless of size, can look bad. There are lots of ways for a place to be bad. But no matter how hopeless a place looks, if there are cats around, it's probably one of the good places. You'll say I'm prejudiced, because of my name. Probably. But if there's even one cat sitting in the sun and looking bored, it's a good guess that the people who live in that place have enough humanity to look after one another and a little left over for the cats.

Fountains has cats. Dogs too, also a good sign, but not as dependable. The entire town is two rows of boxy buildings set parallel to the river. Most of the sturdiest buildings are made of cement blocks, the kind where the windows are made of wavy glass bricks. Great idea, those bricks, until you need to open a window. The fountain the town is named for is an artesian well in the center of town. There's a brick building to house the pipes, so you can't see anything that looks like a fountain. The water comes up pure, an endless stream that tastes of iron. Between the straggle of buildings and the river, Fountains has a levee of big stones cemented together. In the middle of the levee there's a steel shank set into the cement. The shank holds a steel ring as thick as my wrist and as big around as a soup kettle. That ring is perfect for the *River Rat*'s mooring line. Two things make Fountains a regular stop on our travels: the clean water and the levee.

We were already tied up there when I got out on deck. Jake and Lindy were at the bow rail, swinging the landing stage over to the levee. No one was there, unless you count a yellow cat sleeping on a bale of straw. At the far end of the levee, dropping little rocks into the river, two kids were trying to pretend they weren't dying to get a close look at us.

Toby had her mail packet ready. She was ashore with it a moment after the planks of the landing stage were in place. Jake left Lindy coiling line and followed Toby. He doesn't like to let her go ashore alone. Toby has been looking after herself a lot longer than she's known Jake, but she doesn't seem to mind his company. She keeps on with what she's doing, and Jake just strolls along after. They don't say much, even to each other; they don't seem to need to.

Before Toby and Jake were out of sight, Spike had emerged from the engine room to help Lindy with the doctor. That's the contraption used to pump enough water into the boilers to keep us from exploding when we tie up. Esteban was still up in the pilothouse.

The kids had stopped dropping rocks into the river and were watching eagerly. Escaping steam makes a great noise. Very ominous.

The cat was asleep.

So I was the only one who saw the old man come down the steps from the texas deck.

I was at the stern, coiling line, when I caught a movement out of the corner of my eye. The old guy came down the steps without making a sound. He moved quickly and softly across the deck before I could open my mouth. As he measured the gap

2 1

from the rail to the levee, I saw that he carried Lindy's twelve-string guitar on his back.

I yelled, "Hey!" and dropped my line.

The old guy stepped neatly over the rail and jumped ashore. I vaulted the gap and went after him.

The kids watched us go. The cat slept on. I followed the old guy at a distance of maybe thirty yards as he trotted through Fountains. No one paid the slightest attention.

I ought to have shouted for Spike. Or I could have called to Lindy, "Well, hero, there goes the old guy you rescued. He's taking your guitar to remember you by." Instead I just chased him. When I asked Lindy about it later, she said, "Oh, we looked around for you when we finished, but I just thought you were trying to get out of cooking supper." It figures.

So I ran after the guy. The street in Fountains is like a dark gray jigsaw puzzle, old asphalt crumbled by winter and summer weather. It took concentration to hurry along it without tripping. After the first six blocks, the old man snatched a look over his shoulder at me, did a double take, and almost went down. He got his balance and managed another look as he increased his speed. It was as if he didn't believe his eyes.

After his swim he couldn't have been in very good shape for a cross-country run. Jake and Lindy's water rescue alone would have been enough to put me flat for a couple of days. I figured I could catch the guy any time I wanted to, knock him down, take the guitar, and return it to Lindy. It would be tricky to keep from damaging the guitar, but I figured I could manage.

The thing is, I was mad. Lindy had rescued him. Lindy had persuaded Toby to let us keep him as a passenger, at least for a few hours. And not only did he leave without bothering to thank her, he stole her guitar.

So instead of doing the sensible thing, I set my sights on running the old guy to a standstill. I picked my distance just right, not close enough to scare him, not far enough to lose him. I put my head down and watched my steps. It was simple to match his pace. Barring a few soundings, I hadn't done any actual work all day. As I ran, I made my plan. I'd keep after him until he couldn't run anymore. When he was sitting in the middle of the road, fighting to get a good lungful of air, I'd pluck Lindy's guitar away. Then, without a word, I would just turn around and run back to the *River Rat*.

Well, it seemed like a good idea at the time.

Out of town the road runs up toward the bluffs overlooking the river. It's a winding road, not steep at first but long. By the time we were halfway up the slope, the old man was walking. I kept a steady fifty yards behind him and tried to frown constantly because every six steps or so he would glance back at me, scared. Two-thirds of the way up the hill, he came to a fork in the road. He took the downhill slope, even though it was overgrown with brush. The slope helped his speed, and I picked up my pace to keep him in sight as the road made an elbow turn and stopped.

There was a chunk missing from the side of the hill, a stone quarry that looked as though part of the bluff had been blown away. On three sides were walls of sheer rock, butter yellow limestone streaked red with clay. At the bottom of the hole was a sheet of water so still that the walls of the quarry it reflected were complete in every detail. Heaps of stones were everywhere, boulders piled up like pillows, and the old man ran to one before he turned to face me. The look on his face reminded me of a dog that's been kicked, a little mean, a little scared, but mostly uncertain.

I came toward him thinking, What would Jake do? I kept my face as expressionless as I could but held out my hand as I approached him. Nothing threatening. Very neutral, very cool.

Maybe I am not as big as Esteban or Jake. Maybe I am not as fierce as Toby or as plain dangerous as Lindy. But there was no reason in the world why the old guy's face should have cleared as I approached. When I was two steps away, he was almost smiling. He held the twelve-string out to me.

"You're after this," he said. It wasn't a question. "Take it and get out of here, kid."

I frowned at him as I took the guitar.

Now, it would have been sensible to turn around and leave. It would probably even have been what Jake would do. I wish I could say that I did the sensible thing. But the instant the old guy told me to take the guitar and go, that became the very last thing in the world I intended to do.

"Why steal it if you don't want it?" I asked. I ran my fingers over the guitar, found no damage anywhere. "Why run away?"

The old guy stopped almost smiling. "I hope you run faster than I do. You're going to need to get out of here real quick."

"Why?"

"I'm not safe to be around," he replied. "Go on. Get."

"Why aren't you safe to be around?"

The old guy just looked at me. In the silence, not far off, I heard a hound barking.

For a moment, looking at him face to face, I thought I'd been wrong about his age. When I first saw him, I'd guessed he was fifty or even older. Talking to him, I realized he wasn't nearly that old. But when he turned his head, trying to judge the direction the sound was coming from, his age returned. The gleam of humor behind his eyes was gone. He looked old and tired, at least forty, maybe more.

The quarry walls made it hard to tell what direction the hound was coming from, but the possibilities were limited. The old man ran back the way we'd come, through the brush that overgrew the quarry entrance. I slung Lindy's twelve-string over my shoulder and ran after him.

One thing about the bluffs on the upper river, they may not look high, but they are. Steep, too. When we left, the old man took a sharp turn to skirt the lower edge of the quarry. He picked his way, panting, among rocks, trees, and bushes like he knew where he was going. I should've known better. He was just running away from the sound his hunters made, the same way he'd run into the river.

I didn't know better. Instead I followed him through the trees, through briars that tore at my arms and face, through brush that snared my ankles and buckled my knees. If I'd had both hands free to hurry with, I might well have fallen and rolled clear to the bottom, bashing my brains out on a stray boulder. I didn't have both hands free. I had Lindy's twelve-string to carry. I struggled along slowly with one hand out in front of me to catch at tree trunks as I stumbled. The other was clamped in a death grip on the neck of Lindy's guitar. If I could have hurried, I would have. Instead I couldn't seem to take a step without looping a bramble around my neck or stepping on stones rolled loose from the quarry.

Before I took three steps, the old man was out of sight in the undergrowth ahead. I heard the hound behind me, closer.

25

I stepped on yet another rock and fell backward among the brambles and bracken. As I went down I twisted frantically to spare the guitar. I fetched up with my head scraped hard against the white, papery trunk of a birch tree. I managed to avoid landing on the guitar. I buried my face in the crook of my arm, made myself take a long deep breath, and tried to think invisible thoughts. It occurred to me to be glad it wasn't later in the year. If all the trees had lost their leaves, I would have been easy to spot, even flat in the brush.

As I have often noticed, as soon as I closed my eyes, my hearing seemed to get better. I could hear, over my own breathing, the diminishing crash of the old guy's progress down the hill. There were footsteps, men walking close to my right and farther away to my left. I heard the hound approach, a light step and quick panting breath. If the hunters had split up to hurry down the hillside after the old guy, they might miss me completely. If only one found me, I could probably manage to get away somehow.

Intent on the scent he pursued, the hound passed me in the underbrush. The footsteps got faint. Then came a shout and a crash of branches. I pushed myself up on my elbows and reached for the rock I had tripped over last.

Downhill I saw the old man. The hound had brought him to bay at an outcrop and was now clinging grimly to the sleeve of his coat. Under their feet the butter-colored limestone made a ledge. Beyond the ledge lay a sheer drop to the valley below. I caught a glimpse of the old guy's face as he looked up at the pursuers closing in. He was paler than ever, since Lindy had scrubbed the grime off his face, and he looked sick.

There were three of them, all big, all with cudgels. They slowed down when they saw they had him trapped, as if they wanted to make things last. Broad-built, skin reddened by wind and sun, they wore dirt-colored clothes, dark pants and drab shirts that blended with the colors of the hillside.

The old man struggled. He flung his arms wide, trying to shake the hound away. Fabric ripped, and his sleeve came free. The dog fell back. Quick as a snake striking, the old man took the hound's throat between his hands. For a moment I thought he was trying to wring its neck. The hound twisted, snarled, then yelped and struggled in the old man's grasp. Instead of fighting to maintain his grip, the old man flung the hound from him. The lean yellow body twisted in the air and was gone. From far below, where the slope of the bluff met the valley floor, came a muffled crash. There was a long, awful, screaming yelp. I closed my eyes tight for a moment.

The closest pursuer uttered a deep snarl like the dog's and pounced on the old man. I saw the old guy's hands close on the thick wrists, slide free, and try to tighten again. The man had the old guy by the lapels of his rotting coat, had pulled him clear of the ground so his toes scraped the ledge.

The rock in my hand was rough and cold, about the size of an apple. Kneeling is no way to pitch, but I threw it without taking aim, without even thinking. It hit the man square in the back of the head. In its own way it made a nastier sound than the dog had. He let the old man drop, then fell limp on the ledge.

The second pursuer was on the old guy before I could find another rock. The third was starting back up the slope toward me, face red with rage, as I dropped into the brambles. I took a careful sidestep on hands and knees and knocked my shoulder against a chunk of rock wedged between a birch tree and a rotten log. It must have rolled there from the quarry above. With my accidental encouragement, it began to move. The third man was coming up after me, just a little too fast to dodge. The rock bounced toward him. He hesitated, trying to judge when to step out of its way, and it rolled squarely into his left kneecap. He made a terrible sound of rage and pain and went down swearing.

At the very edge of the outcrop, the old man struggled with the second thug. For a moment, as I was scrambling to my feet, yanking at the strap to steady the guitar on my shoulder, I thought the old man would be strangled there on the rim of stone. Then I realized that the second guy was trying to hold him back as the old man fought to go over the edge.

The fellow who'd had his knee smashed threw a fist-sized stone in my direction. It hit the tree beside me, scattering bits of bark that stung my cheek. I stooped, found the stone, and pitched it at him with everything I had. It hit him in the shoulder and raised a little puff of dust from his shirt. He ducked and scrabbled for more stones. I glanced back at the old man and tried to pick the best path down to him. In that moment, as I tried to think how to reach him in time to help, he went limp. As his knees buckled, he threw himself sideways, and the pair of them fell over the ledge locked in each other's arms.

The crippled pursuer yelled and so did I. We both moved toward the ledge. Before we finished the first step, we heard the crash of brush below. There was a scream, another crash, then silence.

It took eight of the guitar's nine lives and a lot of the skin off my knuckles and knees, but I was down the rock face long before the crippled hunter could hobble after me.

I found the old guy snagged in a clump of sumac, a huddled lump of rags. The other man was tangled up with him, but he had landed under the old guy and was dead, his head dangling on his shoulder at a bad angle. The old man was still breathing. I pulled his arms and legs straight and gave him a little shake. After a moment he feebly batted me away. I sat back on my heels and studied him while I caught up on my breathing. He opened his eyes and looked around. For a few moments, until he recognized me, I got that sense again that he wasn't old at all.

"I told you I wasn't safe to be around," he said finally. His voice was rough but very thin, like frayed string.

I looked at the dead man he was lying on. "I see that."

Down the slope above us rolled a series of stones dislodged by the injured pursuer. He had a tough job trying to follow us without ruining his other leg.

"I'm leaving," I said. I rose and dusted off what was left of my knees.

The old man started to get up, realized what he was bracing himself against, and went very still. It took some help from me, but the old man finally gained his feet and steadied himself against a nearby poplar. "I thought you said you were leaving," he said.

I looked back uphill. "Why are they chasing you?" I asked.

He regarded me with pained disbelief. "You really don't listen, do you, kid?" He shook his head and pushed away from the tree, taking a line along the slope to his right.

Neither climbing nor descending, he picked his way straight across the hillside, stumbling from tree to tree en route. Ready to catch him, careful of the guitar, I followed slowly. Ever farther behind us came the sounds of the injured man's pursuit, distant but stubborn.

We followed the curve of the slope back to the road. Across the road, we cut through a ravine until we broke free of the tangling underbrush. We emerged at a clearing left bare by some long-gone forest fire, where nothing grew but sunburnt grass, springing crisp from the stony gray soil. There, we came to a halt.

Below us the river valley spread like a map. Silver and green in the late-afternoon sunlight, the river was edged with reeds and sandbars. To the left, south from our bluff, Fountains lay in the curve of the river, its dingy buildings distinct in the angled light. To the right, in the blue distance of the north, the river ran down from Lake Pippin in deep channels between sandbars. Directly below us a rail bed left the east bank of the river to angle halfway across the valley and disappear into brown water. The last trace of the tracks' existence was the twisted metal of piers that punctuated the main channel. The current had dragged metal and concrete into a ruin, all that was left of the old bridge.

I looked from the valley to the old man. He wasn't admiring the view. He was panting and staring back at Fountains. I followed his gaze. I could see trees and buildings. There was the *River Rat* at the levee, elegant ribbons of gray smoke spiraling from her stacks. I shifted Lindy's guitar on my shoulder and opened my mouth. I don't remember what I was going to say. Probably I meant to ask the old man again why the hunters were chasing him. Before I spoke, the *River Rat*'s whistle sounded. That whistle is a horrible shriek of steam power that can be heard nine miles away. The *Rat*'s signal held for ten long seconds, a full-chested scream of noise. When it broke off, the echo bounced up and down the bluffs.

That signal, one long blast, is the one we use when things are bad. When, no matter what else happens, no matter who's not there, the *River Rat* is casting off.

She cast off so smoothly I couldn't see the moment they set her free. First she drifted away from the levee a little. Then the paddle wheel moved, and she drew out into the channel, the river creaming white in her wake. The *River Rat* was headed north, headed upriver, headed away. Without me.

I looked down the hillside, steep as the roof of a house, between me and the river. And I looked down to the ruined railroad track that ran from the bank out into the heart of the river.

I forgot the old man. I forgot his pursuers. I even forgot the guitar. Without a thought for anything but the *River Rat*, I started down the bluff.

3

A WALK IN
THE WATER

MY MEMORY IS NOT ALWAYS RELIABLE. I remember going down that hillside in three steps. Objective evidence (the seat of my jeans) proves I slid most of the way, but I don't remember sliding. I remember running. I remember that as I reached the bottom of the bluff I thought, with the calm simplicity that total fear brings, *Something went wrong in Fountains.*

I remember seeing a branch lying on the path before me. I thought, *Oh, good—sounding pole*, and snatched it up without breaking stride. I remember that I jumped down the last bank above the railroad tracks. Maybe it was an eight-foot drop. I landed with a jar that shot from the soles of my shoes to my teeth. I staggered, caught my balance, and ran on, measuring my stride to match the railroad ties underfoot.

For the first five hundred yards it was almost easy. I even had a chance to snatch a look around as I gauged my footing. The river upstream was empty. The railroad track ran on ahead of me, two straight lines rushing toward a vanishing point. The river downstream gave me a glimpse of the *River Rat*, coming toward me at a steady eighteen beats a minute.

Even over my breathing, I heard footsteps behind me, a stumbling crunch on the gravel between the railroad ties. I didn't spare a glance back at the old guy. The *Rat* was coming.

One hundred yards before the bridge pier, the tracks disappeared into the greasy brown current of the river. I plunged my branch into the water and hit a railroad tie. Here the river was only inches deep. I kept on, dabbing the stick into the water as I went. The river was over my ankles. It was cold and stung my scratches.

The *River Rat* was close enough for me to see Lindy at the upper deck rail. Her blond hair was like a flag in the breeze as she waved at me. Her green sleeves made big swooping arcs of relief and excitement. I remembered the guitar on my back. If I let anything happen to it now, Lindy would kill me.

The *Rat* was heading for the far side of the pier. At the forward deck rail, Jake was ready with my sounding pole. Beyond the wreckage of the bridge piling lay enough deep water to let the *Rat* pick me up. I hoped. I also hoped that the deep water didn't begin much before the pier. I just hate to swim.

I heard splashing behind me and the old man's voice: "Beat it, kid, or we'll miss the boat." I didn't bother to answer. As we waded on, his breathing was loud behind me.

Toby appeared at Jake's elbow, a coil of line over her shoulder. While Jake called off soundings, she tied one end of the line to the deck rail, shook out the slack, and gave the other end of the line a little swing. From the set of her shoulders, I could tell it was the line I use for soundings on the lower river. That line is thirty feet long, with strips of leather to mark off the fathoms, and a lead weight at the end. Toby swung the line slowly as she judged the distance to the piling. Lead is hard to throw any direction but down.

When I got to the piling, the water was past my knees and the current was pushing hard against my legs. I unslung the guitar and handed it back to the old guy. "Here, hold this," I said. I put my palms flat on the top of the pier. I vaulted to the top on my first try. I reached back to help the old guy. He put the guitar in my hand instead. "You hold it," he said, and took a grip to vault up after me. It took him two tries, but he did it without any help from me.

The *Rat* was closer. I could hear Jake call off the soundings. "Quarter less twain." The *Rat* came steadily on. Maybe they were thirty yards downstream. "Ten feet," Jake called. He sounded very neutral, very cool. A few more yards and he drew the pole up again. "Ten feet."

The *Rat* held her course. There was no chance she could draw closer to the piling as she passed. "Ten feet."

Lindy was hanging over the rail of the upper deck. I held up the guitar and saw her eyes widen. That's how close the *Rat* was getting.

I called, "Here, catch," and swung the guitar on its strap, tossing it in an easy arc toward the *Rat*.

Lindy caught it at the top of the arc. She bared her teeth in a grimace as she drew the guitar in and cradled it in her arms. "Tomcat," she snarled, her voice harsh as silk tearing, "that's not funny."

"Here, yourself," said Toby. "Catch." And she tossed me the lead line.

35

I didn't grab it as neatly as Lindy caught the guitar. It hit me in the chest and nearly knocked me clean off the piling. The old guy got a grip on my belt to steady me. Then he took the line away from me. As soon as I got my balance I knelt beside him. I helped him tie the line in a clumsy knot around the likeliest piece of steel. The *River Rat* was nearly abreast of us as I rose and looked into the old guy's face. "If you're going, " I said, "go."

He went, hand over hand along the line.

"Ten feet," said Jake, regular as a clock says tick.

The old man was halfway across. The *River Rat* drew past the piling. The line was taut between the rail and the steel. I saw Toby look down at the rail. I caught her thought as clear as if she'd spoken aloud. She was wondering which would give way first, the lead line or the rail. The old man was still six feet from the *Rat*, but I was almost out of time.

"Hurry up, Tomcat," Lindy called. I looked up and met her green eyes, her crooked, wicked grin. What was the worst thing that could happen? Wasn't it better to drown trying to get there than to let the *Rat* go without me?

I squared my shoulders, shook some tension out of my fingertips, and stepped onto the line.

Time runs so slowly when you're afraid. I had time between my first step and my second to feel the line solid under my feet. I had time between the second step and the third to wonder how long the line would hold. It had the entire weight of the *River Rat* straining upstream against it. I had time between the third step and the fourth to see Jake and Toby drag the old man in over the rail. And I had time to feel the line draw tight beneath me, until it was like standing on a guitar string about to snap. That's when I knew I wouldn't get another step.

36

When the line broke, I was close to the rail. Close enough to pitch forward and hit the rail hard with my chest. I clutched and hung on.

Above me, I heard Lindy's voice, clear and strong. *"Pretty work, brave boys, pretty work, I say,"* she sang.

I would have liked to vault over the rail and land neatly on deck. I wanted to come aboard with a flourish. But all I could do was hang there, panting, until Jake and Toby pulled me in by my jacket collar. I stayed where they dropped me while I got my breath back.

The old man was sitting on the deck too, nursing his hands after his trip across the lead line. I spared him a glance, then looked up at Toby, who was looming over me with her arms crossed, scowling.

"You deserve to be left behind," she said to me. Her voice was calm, but her eyes weren't. I squirmed. "Never do that again."

I shook my head. Toby clapped me on the shoulder, a pat of encouragement. Then, boots thundering on the deck, she stamped over to the old guy. He didn't look up at first. When he did, I could tell from the calm, weary expression on his face that he had no notion of the state she was in.

"You don't ride this ship for free," Toby informed him. Her voice was very soft, almost a murmur.

Jake drew back from another sounding, stole a glance at Toby, and let the pole thump to the deck without calling off the depth. We stared at each other, wide-eyed with alarm. After a moment he collected himself and called, "Ten feet."

Toby ignored him, all her attention on the old guy. Her eyes blazed. "You don't ride this ship at all unless you talk. And you better talk fast," she advised him, ice in her soft voice, "or I will kick you off this deck right now."

Lindy clattered down from the upper deck, sat beside me, and began to tune her twelve-string. It was neither the time nor the place, but tell Lindy that. She would probably quote Esteban: Practice is the best of all instructors. She leaned toward me and whispered, "I'm glad I saw you do that. I never would have believed it if anyone told me." Under her hands, the twelve-string hummed *Pretty work, brave boys, pretty work, I say. Say I'm going away on board a man-o'-war.*

The old man looked back at his hands.

Jake made another sounding, called, "Mark three."

It became very quiet on deck except for Lindy's twelve-string. The old guy kept on looking at his hands. Toby looked at the old guy. Everyone else watched Toby.

"All right," said Toby. She looked at me, abstracted. "What's the depth here, anyway?"

Jake took another sounding. "Mark four," he called. He put the pole down and folded his arms.

Toby turned back to the old guy. "Twenty-four feet of water," she said. "Will that do?"

The old man didn't answer, just looked at the skin of his palms. Under the dirt they were chafed red.

"All right," said Toby. When she spoke again, her voice was so soft I could scarcely catch her words. "Help me, Jake."

She put her hands under the old man's arms. Jake gave Toby a long measuring look, then bent to get the old guy's ankles. When he straightened, Jake's face was wiped clean of all expression. That's the way Toby always tries to look. She always fails.

Between them, Toby and Jake lifted the old man off the deck. They took a step toward the rail.

I leaned to whisper to Lindy. "What happened in Fountains, anyway?"

Lindy leaned close to reply, so close I caught the scent of her hair. "About fifteen minutes after Jake and Toby left," she whispered, "this bunch of guys showed up. Big guys, red faces, brown shirts. They were looking for somebody. They thought they were going to search the *Rat*, until the dog they had with them began to bark. Then they split into two groups. One group went with the dog. The rest stayed with the *River Rat*. Toby and Jake came back, and the guys tried to stop them. And Esteban came down to say he had seen more guys headed our way. Jake said if we were going to make our exit at all, we had to do it then. Toby and I argued, but Esteban agreed with Jake. Pretty soon Esteban and Jake persuaded Toby. I got outvoted. Sorry."

I shrugged. "So these red-faced guys just let you go."

"Not exactly," said Lindy. She reached up to smooth the crest of her pale hair back out of her eyes and toward her right ear. She does that when she's pleased with herself. "There was a brief scuffle."

"I'll bet," I said. "Is that what got Toby so mad?"

"Esteban hurt his arm in the fight. It's all bruised and swollen and sort of crooked. He's steering fine with the other, though."

From within Toby and Jake's embrace the old man said, "Sounds like a fracture to me."

"You shut up," said Toby. She had backed up until the old guy's head was over the rail. Jake was still holding his ankles, but

39

he was looking less impassive and more embarrassed by the second.

"You told me to talk," the old man reminded Toby. Slung between them like a dirty hammock, he didn't look alarmed. He didn't even seem very interested, just resigned and a little bored.

For a moment I thought Toby really was going to drop him overboard. Her eyes flashed and her mouth made a thin hard line. Then she swallowed and said, "Talk."

"I think I should take a look at the kid's arm," the old guy said. "After all, the hands of the king are the hands of a healer."

Toby hesitated, then nodded at Jake to release the man's ankles. Jake looked relieved. They let him down on the deck.

"Is that so?" Lindy looked skeptical. "Just what are you supposed to be king of?"

"Nothing. My name is King. It's a saying: 'The hands of the king . . .'" The old guy got slowly to his feet, leaned against the rail for a moment. He sighed and said, "Never mind. Where's the kid with the broken arm?"

"Are you a doctor?" asked Lindy.

King looked down at her for a moment, then sighed again. "No, but I used to go out with one." He shrugged. "Forget it. If you think you can find yourselves a genuine doctor, go right ahead. If all you need is a broken arm set, I can probably help."

Toby eyed him coldly. When she spoke, the last anger was gone from her voice. She sounded tired. "Jake, get him up to the pilothouse. I'll be up to take the wheel in a minute."

"Wouldn't it be better to bring the kid down here?" asked King.

"We can always ask," said Jake.

Lindy grinned up at the old guy. "I don't think Esteban will come down for a little thing like this. He's kind of stubborn."

Jake and King departed, leaving Toby looming over Lindy and me. By this time Lindy was just working her way up and down the guitar's scales. It sounded like somebody tiptoeing up and down stairs very quickly.

Toby eyed me, frowning. "What's that stuff on your forehead?"

I reached up to touch my forehead. Dried blood flaked away on my hand, and I remembered the birch tree. "Nothing," I said. "I'm fine."

"Well, then," Toby said, "what were you thinking of, to take off alone like that?"

It would have been easier to tell the story if Lindy hadn't been sitting right beside me, highly entertained. I did my best to explain why I decided to retrieve the guitar and finished up with, "It seemed like a good idea at the time. It could have been worse."

"Well, that's true," said Lindy. "At least you didn't get a legful of porcupine quills this time."

I ignored that remark and kept my attention on Toby.

Toby sighed. "Enough. You saw them too. What do you think? Why are they chasing him?"

I shook my head. "They're hunting both sides of the river. They must have a good reason to go to all that trouble. Ask the old guy again."

Toby took her eyes off mine, which was a relief to me, and looked up at the pilothouse. Her expression was a perfect balance of suspicion and worry. "I will," she said, "after he sets Esteban's arm."

"It might not even be broken," said Lindy. "That Lester only hit him once."

"You go help Spike," said Toby. "We're making the run to Red's Landing before we tie up tonight. I don't want those Lesters catching us while Esteban's laid up. Spell Spike while the light lasts. And, Tomcat? Wash your face." She left us to climb to the pilothouse.

I rose stiffly and reached down to give Lindy a hand. She got up without it, still working on her scales. Together we headed for the engine room. "What's a Lester?" I asked her.

"Those red-faced guys," said Lindy. "The leader had one of those shirts with a name embroidered on the pocket. That was the name."

"What kind of name is that?" I asked.

"What do you think the old guy did to make them so mad?" countered Lindy. "Why should they want to kill him?"

I remembered the struggle on the outcrop when the old man fought until his opponent went over the edge with him. "Are you sure they want to kill him?"

"Well, if they don't," replied Lindy, "they want to catch him pretty bad."

"He wants to get away pretty bad," I said. I remembered how he'd looked in the quarry when he'd heard the pursuit behind us. "Real bad."

Lindy took over in the engine room. Spike reluctantly let her, but not until he dispatched me to the pilothouse with a message about fireboxes. That's why I was there when it became clear that Lindy's guess had been right. Esteban refused to leave the pilothouse while the *River Rat* was under way, and he refused any suggestion that we put in to shore before we reached Red's Landing.

"One must roam in the world as a lion of self-control," said Esteban stubbornly.

"Great," said King. Gently he explored Esteban's injured right wrist. "You get to be a lion of self-control right here and now." He showed Jake and Toby where to hold Esteban's arm.

This left me to hold the wheel, steering the *River Rat* on a steady course upstream while they set Esteban's broken arm. I hardly ever get a chance to navigate. I tried to make the most of it, but the sound Esteban made at the crucial moment spoiled any pleasure I had. I swallowed hard and kept my hands as steady as I could on the smooth wood of the wheel. I could feel the pulse of the ship through my fingertips.

"How's that?" asked King. "Any better? How did you break it, anyway? That's a nasty bruise." He wound bandages around the splint, his grimy fingers deft with the strips of cloth.

Jake took up a bludgeon slung from a leather thong. It had been left on the bench at the back of the pilothouse, a piece of polished wood with a heft that betrayed a lead weight somewhere inside. "One of the Lesters had this. Esteban took it away from him."

"You took that and then he broke your arm?" King asked Esteban respectfully.

Jake lifted his eyebrows. "Oh, no. The Lester broke his arm and *then* he took it away from him."

Esteban took a step forward and joined me at the wheel. For a moment his hand rested on the wood between mine. The wooden wheel eased in my grasp as though his touch soothed it.

Then I stepped aside and let Esteban have the wheel to himself. Bandaged arm held stiff at his side, he seemed to guide the *River Rat* effortlessly with one hand. Eyes on the channel ahead, expression demure, Esteban spoke in a voice touched with smugness. "Don't let the frogs of sense weakness kick you around."

Jake began to gather up bandages.

"Are you all right, Esteban?" Toby asked.

Esteban nodded without taking his eyes off the river.

Toby turned to the old man, who sank down on the bench with a sigh. "Right, then," she said. "Talk."

King shook his mud-colored hair back over his shoulders and looked up at Toby. "It's a funny thing," he observed. "Every time you order me to talk, I get this overpowering urge to beat around the bush."

"I noticed that," said Toby dryly.

King shrugged. "You want it in my own words? Or is this a formal confession?"

"Who are those Lesters?" asked Toby. "What do they want from you?"

"They think I have something they want," King replied.

Jake and Toby watched the old man as if they could stare him into continuing, or as if they could tell by looking whether or not he was lying to us. I glanced around, from Esteban, who was absorbed by the river, to Jake and Toby, back to King, and decided to curl up on the deck. This was going to take a while.

"And do you have it?" asked Toby.

King shrugged. "If I had it, I'd let them take it."

"Who are they?" asked Toby.

King shrugged again. "You saw them. You know what they are. Small bullies with ambition. They want to be big bullies."

"Why did you take Lindy's guitar?" I asked.

Everybody glared at me but Esteban.

The old guy frowned. "That was a mistake." He looked back at Toby. "Look. If you want to put me over the side, do it. If you want to put me ashore someplace, do it. To tell you the truth, it doesn't make a hell of a lot of difference to me. Face it, you haven't got a lever that will move me."

"Tough talk," said Jake very softly.

King shifted his gaze from Toby to Jake. His frown turned into an expression of faint amusement. "When you're my age, you'll know what's talk and what isn't. If you want a lesson now, that's fine with me. Put it to the test."

It was Jake's turn to look amused. "That's tough talk, too."

King laughed. "There's more where that came from. When you get tired of listening, there's a simple solution to all your problems. Just let me go."

"Talk first," said Toby.

King shook his head. "If you insist, you can turn me over to them the next time they ask. But I'd consider it a favor if you gave me five minutes' notice before you do that."

"Five minutes' notice so you can jump in the river again," I said.

Everyone but Esteban looked at me, but this time they didn't glare.

"You saw the old guy go in the river," I continued, glancing from King to Toby. "I saw him go over the edge of the bluff. He's right about not caring anymore. But there's one thing that doesn't fit — Lindy's guitar."

King looked pained. "I am starting to wish I'd never seen that thing."

"Good," I said. "Same here. Why take it if you really don't care what happens to you? And why just give it back to me?"

King lifted his shoulders slightly. "I don't know. I didn't see any reason to destroy it. Maybe you don't realize how valuable something like that is."

"Oh, we realize," I said.

Toby said, "Tomcat's got a point. Why did you take it?"

King shrugged. "It reminded me of the way things used to be. I used to play guitar, back before the Flash. When I saw it, I just . . . I just made a mistake. If you want a formal apology, I apologize. I apologize for your arm, too, kid," he said to Esteban. "But remember, none of this would have happened if you'd left me in the river."

"So this is all someone else's fault," I said. "That figures."

"If you won't tell us why you're being pursued," said Esteban, eyes still on the river, "perhaps you will tell us how far they will pursue you."

King threw up his hands. "I thought they'd give up miles back. Where are we, anyway?"

"About nine miles south of Alma," Esteban replied. "That's Twenty-Mile Point up ahead. No snags after that. With the full moon, we'll make it to Red's Landing with no trouble."

Toby joined Esteban at the wheel. "You get us past Twenty-Mile Point. I'll take it from there. You can get some rest."

"I don't want any rest," Esteban replied. His arm must have been bothering him. He can usually think of a much longer way to say something like that.

I won't describe the whole argument. Esteban stayed stubborn. Toby finally agreed to let him stay at the helm until we reached Red's Landing, on condition that he leave the pilothouse the moment we tied up. Further, given the chance of pursuit from the Lesters, we would post a sentinel in the pilothouse. We would take turns watching all night long to be certain King brought us no unexpected company.

"Tomcat will take first watch," said Jake. "He can turn in early afterward. He needs to be up first to fix breakfast, anyway."

I actually don't mind cooking. But if I said so, I suspect I'd get assigned some other chore instead. And chances are I wouldn't like the other chore as much. That's why I pretend I don't like to cook. Esteban tells a story about a rabbit and a briar patch that gave me the idea originally. So I made a fairly disgusting face, which reminded Toby that I still had dried blood on my forehead.

"I know," I told her, "but you keep giving orders. How am I supposed to cook and shovel coal and carry messages *and* wash?"

Jake cleared his throat. "And how is it that somehow you aren't doing *any* of those things?" he asked.

I decided to leave before they thought of more little jobs for me, and headed down to the galley. After all, there was nothing more to do in the pilothouse but watch Esteban be stubborn until we reached Red's Landing.

Supper was lentil soup. I don't mean to brag, but I make pretty good lentil soup. The tricky part is remembering to add water every so often to keep it from setting up like mortar in the bottom of the kettle. I thinned out a bowl and took it to Lindy in the engine room.

"Thanks. How's Esteban?" asked Lindy, putting the shovel away and accepting the soup.

"Same as ever," I said. "Good thing his arm is in a splint. I think Toby would have slugged him otherwise."

47

Lindy pointed her spoon at me. "Let me guess. He told her one must roam in the world as a lion of self-control."

"Yeah, he was being pretty stubborn," I said. "When we put in at Red's Landing, Toby will get her revenge by tucking him into his bunk."

"Not likely," said Lindy, scraping the bowl.

BY THE TIME Spike returned to the engine room, the moon was well up. I watched it from the starboard rail as we came to Red's Landing. It hung over the bluffs across the river, its reflection a sulfur-yellow smear on the dark water.

Red's Landing was probably never much more than a wide spot in the road. Once the road was a highway, paralleling the river. Now it's broken concrete edged with goldenrod and milkweed. Trees come down the hillside as far as the road, but from there it's open ground to the landing, very reassuring to any sentinel posted in the pilothouse. The river runs deep right up to the landing, very reassuring to anyone with a sounding pole.

Jake and I tied up at our favorite tree stump. I climbed to the pilothouse and took first watch. Lindy sat with me just to keep me company. I stood at the wheel, resting my hands on the cool wood. Behind me on the bench, Lindy worked on one of her practice pieces. She hadn't let the guitar out of her sight since I'd brought it back. The piece had a lot of strange minor chords. She kept playing it over and over, a little faster each time.

I listened as I looked ashore to the moonlit clearing, then out at the moonlit spaces of the river. Big and still, the moon bleached the bright stars. Lovely on the water, it lit the river in shifting patterns of black and silver. Every pattern was slightly different, every pattern made and remade itself, flowing like silk in the wind.

It was a good thing Lindy was with me or I would have fallen asleep for sure.

Jake came for the middle watch to let Lindy and me go to our cabins on the texas deck. King was with him.

"I'm keeping him close," Jake explained as he took my post at the lifeless wheel. "We thought about locking him in a cabin for safekeeping, but I'd rather have him where I can see him."

"Cruel and unusual punishment," said King. "Do you expect me to sleep right here on the deck?"

"This is guard duty. I don't expect you to sleep at all," said Jake. "You can sit on the bench if you get tired."

"I understand," I said. "If you let him have a cabin, he'd be a passenger, wouldn't he? Can't have that. This way he's practically a member of the crew."

"Well, if I have to sit here, at least give me something to do," said King. He put out his hand to Lindy. "Take pity on a man who remembers the world as it was before the Flash. Let me borrow your guitar."

For a long moment Lindy was entirely still. There was nothing to hear in the pilothouse but the constant murmur of the river. Then Lindy let her breath go softly and held out the guitar. "Just for tonight," she said. "Because I'd hate to want music and not be able to make any."

The old man ducked his head as he accepted the guitar. "A gracious gesture. Thank you."

Lindy gave him a nod in return. She left the pilothouse without saying good night.

When I finally put my head down on my own thin pillow, I was too tired to yawn myself into a comfortable position. I lay limp while my knees reminded me of what I'd done all day. The scratches on my hands and ankles, the bruises on my elbows, and the scrape on my forehead chimed in. Thanks to the sounding pole and the coal shovel, even my shoulder blades ached. I felt a little sorry for myself.

Then, out of the hush of the river, so softly that at first I thought I was imagining it, I heard someone playing the guitar. It was Lindy's practice piece. Somehow I knew it wasn't Lindy playing. The music was slow and easy, sweet and gloomy. It made me forget my aches and pains. Instead it made my heart feel bruised. It was a strange feeling, to be sad for nothing, for no reason I could think of, just for the sound of the music.

I kicked off my blanket. It was stupid to let a practice piece of Lindy's make me feel bad. I'd go ask the old guy to play something else. Before I got out of my bunk, the music stopped. Sitting still in the dark, all I could hear was the sound the river made. I pulled up the blanket and lay back listening for a long time, but he didn't play any more.

4

LOITERING
WITH INTENT

AT SUNUP THE NEXT MORNING, THERE WAS a mist on the river. On my way down to get a shovelful of coals to start the galley stove, I paused at the aft rail. As I watched, the mist rose from the water in faint wisps and twists, so white it seemed blue in the early light. Like smoke, it masked the river.

While I looked, King came to stand beside me at the rail. I gave him a sidelong glance. He ignored me, leaned on his elbows, and gave the view a grunt that might have meant his back hurt.

"Where's Jake?" I asked.

King shrugged. "Asleep."

I looked toward the shore. "Then isn't this your big chance?" I asked. "Go on, old guy. Make your getaway. Who'd see you go?"

King spat over the rail. "This fog won't last. Nothing this lovely ever lasts."

"Who'd chase you?" I asked. "Anyway, it wouldn't be the same if it lasted. If it lasted, it'd be weather and people would complain about it. It's better like this, just river smoke."

"I suppose you're young enough for that to make sense," King said patiently. "You'll change your mind when you're older."

"I hate it when people tell me I'll change when I get older," I said. "Disagree with me if you want, but don't put it down to my age. That's like saying I'm too stupid to have a valid opinion."

"Don't get so excited, kid," said King. "When I was your age, I was stupid myself."

"But you've changed," I replied. I put as much sarcasm into the words as I could, but it didn't seem to be enough for King to notice.

"Yeah," said King and shrugged. He had a shrug for every occasion.

I pointed to shore. "Why don't you leave? Yesterday you asked us to let you go."

"I changed my mind," said King, without taking his eyes from the mist on the river. "When did you kids vote to let me go?"

"It's a notion of my very own," I replied. "Are you going to change your mind again when we get you farther away from the Lesters? Why are you so scared of them, anyway? They don't have any power over you. If you really aren't afraid to die, no one has any power over you."

King raised his eyebrows. "Do you all talk like the lion of self-control?" He gave a little jerk of his head to indicate the pilothouse. "He's up there right now, just sitting there, watching the river. He took the watch from Jake — said the moon was too bright to let him sleep. It's his arm hurting, of course."

"Are you trying to change the subject?" I asked.

King ignored me. "There, what did I tell you?" I followed his gaze. The mist was gone. The morning sun burned silver on the shifting current. "I knew it wouldn't last."

"Hey, Tomcat," Spike called down from the texas deck, "the stove's out. Are we going to get anything to eat or not?"

"What's your hurry?" I retorted. "It's only oatmeal." I turned back to King, but the old guy was headed up to join Spike. I shook my head and went after the coals.

Nobody likes oatmeal. But say what you want, oatmeal lasts. For one thing, no one ever asks for seconds. My only complaint about the stuff is scrubbing the pot out afterward.

We were under way long before I was finished in the galley. By the time I had the bowls and spoons clean, the oatmeal in the pot had turned to slime and of course the wash water was cold again. I use sand to scrub with. Between the cold water, the sand, and the oatmeal slime, I scraped open every scratch on my hands. Still, sand is a lot cheaper than cake soap. And it rinses off faster, too. That bubble soap people used to have must have been rough to rinse off. I've seen pictures in books, of people in bathtubs, for example, where the bubble soap is just thick as a blanket. How did they ever get that off so they could get clean? With sand you know where you are at. If you've got any, you still need to scrub. If you don't, your dishes are clean.

By the time I pitched the dirty wash water over the rail, we were far away from Red's Landing.

"Nice try, Tomcat," Jake called up from the main deck. "You almost got me that time."

I leaned far out over the rail to look down at him. "Why aren't you taking soundings?"

"Look around," said Jake. He lifted his arm to sketch the broad channel over the rail. "No bottom. We're in Lake Pippin."

I followed his gesture. It's difficult to tell where Lake Pippin begins. The river runs through it. Only the bluffs on either side suggest the boundary. They seem to draw back and get smaller as the river widens into the lake. From the heart of Lake Pippin the bluffs look as small as riverbanks. No bottom to trouble the *River Rat* there: the lake is so deep the water looks like ink. But the surface is always choppy, no matter how still the weather.

I came down to the main deck and found Jake, Toby, Lindy, and King together in deep debate over the instruments. Toby had insisted we play at our next landing, Bass City, to earn enough food to keep us off oatmeal for a while. Jake and Lindy agreed, but they couldn't come to terms on how to arrange the music while Esteban was out with his broken arm.

King looked up from the amplifier Lindy was showing him to ask, "What does he play, anyway?"

Lindy looked up at him, a gleam in her eyes. "Rhythm guitar," she answered. Her mouth quirked just a little. "I play lead, of course."

King gave her a mocking nod. "Oh, of course." He glanced at Toby, then at Jake. "Maybe I could double for him, just this once." He took Esteban's guitar out of its case. "This it?"

Toby's eyes narrowed. But Lindy was already helping King with cables.

"Where's the juice?" asked King, just as Jake flicked the canvas away from the bank of Lovich Chargeables. For a split second King's eyes widened. Then he burst out laughing.

Lindy plugged in the amp and gave King a reproachful look. "Well, they work," she said. She sounded defensive.

King drew in a deep unsteady breath of wonder and amusement. "I just never saw so many Never Readies in one place before, that's all. My, my. Twenty pounds apiece and what do they give you? Nine volts each?"

Lindy shook her hair back and looked scornful. "We do a little better than that."

"And you recharge them with steam, is that it?" King's shoulders shook very slightly, but he was able to keep his voice steady.

"Not quite," said Jake dryly. He traded looks with Toby.

King finished laughing and picked up Esteban's guitar. "As long as it works," he said, shaking his head. He selected a pick from the case and drew it hard across the metal strings. The sound it made was faint and sour. "So you sing for your supper. How am I supposed to tune this thing if you don't turn it on?"

"We don't have the power to waste practicing," said Lindy. "We tune and then we play."

King shrugged. "I guess there isn't much sense in practicing if you're only going to play for people who pay you with creamed corn."

"If we need it and they have it, what difference does it make what we play for?" asked Lindy.

"It makes no difference to you," Toby told him. "You're playing for free."

King's lip curled to show yellowed teeth. "Oh, am I?"

Toby nodded. "You cost us half a tank of fresh water back there in Fountains. Jake says you promised to stay aboard unguarded, but you still don't ride for free. You're playing for your passage."

King tossed his pick back into the guitar case. "No tuning, no practice, no pay. This job stinks."

Toby shrugged. I was glad to see she did it with even more expression than King. "We wouldn't accomplish anything with a single rehearsal, anyway. Lindy, go over the song list with him. Make sure he knows all the chords." She headed for the upper deck.

I caught Jake's expression as he watched her go. I could tell he knew King could play all the chords. Anyone who had heard King play Lindy's guitar would know that. Jake glanced at King and Lindy, who had their heads together over the open guitar case. He looked at me and shrugged.

"You too, Jake?" I looked at King. He was listening to Lindy and looking bored. "Pretty soon he'll have us all doing it."

Jake looked down at me, curious. "Doing what?"

I shrugged elaborately.

Jake grinned. "Oh."

YOU CAN TELL from the roads that Bass City used to be more than just a village. One road runs along the eastern shore of the river. The other runs along the Rupert River, which comes down out of a fertile little valley to meet the big river. Where the roads meet, there are gray metal towers, storage bins for grain. Once those bins were full. Now they anchor the walls of Bass City, a tower at each corner of a wooden stockade. Bass City is one of the good places, with cats and dogs both. But the work it takes to keep a place good is hard. When there's a reason to take a holiday, and the *River Rat* is always a reason, the whole town comes down to the levee. The older people say they only come for the mail. The little kids come to stare at us and drop small rocks in the river. Everyone else comes for the music. Maybe they don't like all the songs we play, but it's still better than weeding beets. A few miles out Esteban gave them a note on the *Rat*'s steam whistle. By the time we put in, at midday, we had a big crowd at the levee, maybe sixty or seventy people.

We always try to give the crowd something to stare at. Under a brown jacket with the sleeves ripped out, Lindy was wearing her favorite shirt of grass green silk. She thinks the color matches her eyes, but she's wrong. Her eyes are darker green, like sunlight in the shallows of the river. Not that I've ever told her so.

Not much of Spike was visible behind the drum kit. He was fixing the angle of one of the drums, but there wasn't anything really wrong with it. He straightened for a moment, and I saw he'd changed into a purple T-shirt under a leather vest. Another moment and he was down on the deck fussing with some cables. Spike rearranges the drums right up until Toby's downbeat. It keeps him from getting nervous.

Jake had taken off his coat to play keyboards in his shirt-sleeves. I was glad he and Lindy were well apart because his shirt was red-and-black check. The strain of looking back and forth between Lindy's green and his checks made my eyes twinge. I blinked and looked over at Toby. You can always count on Toby to wear something nice and drab. This time she was just dressed in her usual oversized black, but her top hat had a rakish tilt.

No one ever pays any attention to me behind the control

board, but I changed into my best shirt and combed my hair anyway. Spike is willing to trust me with the board. All the settings are plainly marked, and even he has to admit I'll never do any damage to the *River Rat* with it. I stay behind the board because if I sing, you can tell why they call me Tomcat. It's not that I can't sing, exactly. It's that no one can stand to listen to me for very long.

Esteban was up in the pilothouse and refused to come down. I'd asked him if he was still keeping sentinel in case of Lesters, but he gave me the oneness-of-existence speech until I said I had to go find my comb.

The old guy looked terrible. He was wearing the same ragged overcoat he'd swum in, open over a frayed gray undershirt that proved even a thin man can have a potbelly. He seemed surprised by the size of our audience and depressed by how orderly they were.

As usual Lindy made a big production out of tuning. She's the best of us all at putting on a show. There is something in her wild, wicked smile that makes the audience feel like her conspirators. What she does is tune for a while and then pause. The rest of the Rats sigh and smile and make a feint at the first chord. Lindy starts to tune again. The rest of the Rats take turns looking irritated. Lindy mugs to the crowd and goes through it all again with variations. The crowd loves it. By the time she was well under way, the crowd had settled quietly into their places. Lindy got her showmanship the same way she learned to fight. Her family followed the fairs north in spring and south in fall, providing every form of entertainment from horse trading to staged sword fights. I don't know why Lindy left the festival road. The only time I ever asked her about it, she laughed. But it wasn't a real laugh, just a fake theatrical one. It curved her mouth and left her eyes sad and a little scared. So I didn't ask again.

By the time the crowd was as thoroughly tuned as Lindy's guitar, she cocked her head and caught Toby's eye. Toby shifted her bass guitar and glanced over to me, then lifted her chin slightly. That's the signal for me to hit the juice. I hit the switches. Our wall of Lovich Chargeables kicked in the carefully hoarded power and the stacks of amplifiers sprang to life with a creaky squeak of feedback.

Toby dropped her chin. The River Rats took her downbeat and noise changed into music.

Sure, the Rats are ragged. Bound to be. They never get to practice with the juice turned on. Sure, the Rats make mistakes. Doesn't everyone? But the Rats are loud. In Bass City, loud is good enough.

The first verse of the opener ("Stick Wizard," my favorite) was as ragged as any song I've ever heard them play. Threads of sound unraveling from the guitars snarled behind Jake's vocals. Spike's backbeat was off for eight bars. King was playing with his chin sunk on his chest, looking too miserable to glance up at the crowd. At the chorus he doubled Lindy's part. At the bridge he made the first half of Lindy's solo an accidental duet.

The crowd didn't care. Some of the boys in the back were on their feet already, and it was only the first number. I watched warily from the control board and wondered if they'd been drinking. Sometimes it's a good thing we have too much equipment to unload from the *River Rat*. We stay aboard with all our gear and play to the riverbank. That way all we need to do to avoid a brawl is slip the cable and push off into the current. It has come in handy more than once.

The last verse of "Stick Wizard" wasn't ragged at all. It sounded good. King's chin was still on his chest, but the miserable look on his face had turned into concentration. There's something wonderful about music. No matter how petty the musician is at heart, when the music has his attention, something takes the pettiness away. I don't mean King looked like a saint or anything, but when he played, there was a light in his face that had never been there before.

All I know about music is the way it makes me feel. I like the way Toby weaves her bass into a net over the beat of Spike's drums. I like the way Jake's simple keyboards tie the background tight and steady and dark. I like the way Lindy's solo guitar cuts across the net and climbs. But best of all I like the way the whole thing hits me, a hot thick wall of sound I can lean on until the music changes my heartbeat to match.

More boys in the back got up for the second number, "Headed for the Angels," and girls got up to dance with them. Dancing is a good sign. Very few fights can match a crowd of people with their hearts set on dancing.

"Headed for the Angels" came out smooth. By the time they got to "Zeitgeist Gals," the Rats were rocking. Jake leaned into the words, a gleam of pure malice in his smile as he took the vocal to the bridge at top speed, then stepped back to let Lindy take the guitar solo.

But Lindy didn't take it. She was watching King's hands on Esteban's guitar, her eyes wide with wonder.

The solo came just the same, plaintive and certain, wailing down the road Jake's deep voice selected, clean and collected from the old guy's hands.

It wasn't Lindy's surprise that made me realize how good King was. It wasn't Jake's gleam of amusement, a look of pure "I thought so." It was the crowd that convinced me. In sixteen bars the crowd went from a group of listeners with a scatter of dancers to a shouting gang of people rocking in unison, swimming in sound.

"Zeitgeist Gals" ended, and "Loitering with Intent" began, but the crazed wail of King's guitar followed without a stumble. The "Loitering" solo was new to me. The solo climbed above the rest of the music, determined as a suicide, high, higher, high enough. When "Loitering with Intent" ended, he didn't let us down. He kept on climbing while the tunes melted into new music.

King had his head up and his shoulders back. He wasn't looking at the crowd. He wasn't looking at anything. His eyes were half shut. If it hadn't been for his hands, if it hadn't been for the music, I would have judged that look of his belonged to a man about to fall asleep.

The crowd would have kept us there all day. Six songs later the lights on my board told me another story. I caught Toby's eye and signaled that the power was starting to go. She gave me a tight little nod. King didn't know our system of head jerks and lifted eyebrows, but he caught the shift in tempo as the music drew toward a close. Together they brought the last song in as the lights before me dimmed. I shut the board down. Suddenly, there was no sound but the crowd. Before that died,

Toby was out on the landing stage, her guitar discarded for the mail sack.

There are never many letters, but the crowd doesn't care. Even one is cause for jubilation. The shouts go on as people bring their payment for the music and the messages: a bushel of apples, another of beets, a chicken, a sack of oatmeal.

All around, the Rats loaded provisions and handled mail. Spike laughed with one of the Bass City kids as he rattled a brisk tattoo out of the deck rail with his drumsticks. Lindy took the chicken, which flapped in her grasp and struggled with the string tethered to its scaly legs. Jake, busy with beets, called advice that Lindy ignored. In the heart of the bustle, chin sunk on his chest, King stood, his hands quiet on the dead guitar. He was so still it seemed like I'd turned him off when I killed the mikes and amps. Silent in the uproar, King lifted his head at last. With gentle hands, he put Esteban's guitar back in its case.

I got up from the control board to coil cables. When I was so close that he couldn't pretend not to hear me, I said, "You played good."

He snapped the case shut and put it aside. "I played great," he said. His face was bleak. "They never even asked for an encore."

"They never do," I said. "No juice."

King's expression lightened. "Oh. I forgot the Never Readies. Well." He shrugged. "Sure is different from the old days."

I looked around. In the sunlight the *River Rat* was poised between the glitter of the river and the glow of autumn in the trees on shore. Beneath me the deck was alive. Above me the decks and steps and railing of the *River Rat* came together in a whole as simple and beautiful as the circuit of a paddle wheel. I wondered how the world could possibly have been any better before the Flash. Finally I shrugged back at King. "I'll bet you complained in the old days too."

Toby handed the mail sack to Jake and turned back to us. "You're up next," she said to me.

Lindy eyed King with new respect. "You sure do know a lot of chords."

Surprised by such limited praise, King said halfheartedly, "Gee, thanks."

"That pays your passage from Fountains to Bass City," Toby said. "You can go ashore here."

"What about the water tanks?" asked King, one eyebrow up.

"After 'Loitering with Intent,' we're even," Toby replied. "Tomcat, get on with it."

Given a choice between showing off and working, I pick showing off every time. So I'm usually the one to stand up in front of the crowd and calm them down with a story, or news, or whatever their mood seems to call for. My contribution to things is designed to quiet the crowd while we pack up and get ready to cast off.

The River Rats are always a tough act to follow, if only because everyone's ears are ringing, but after King and his chords, I knew it would be impossible not to disappoint the audience. So when I took my place on the landing stage, I just gave them the theatrical bow Lindy taught me.

Storytelling comes easy for me. If I can remember to smile and keep my hands out of my pockets, it usually goes pretty well.

The hardest thing is knowing when to stop. Sometimes you can make a good story great just by letting the ending hang while the crowd makes its own reaction. Sometimes you can wreck a good story by going on a few words too long. A really great story will make the crowd beg for more. But don't give it to them, because you can never top yourself, and the crowd will just decide they were wrong and the first story wasn't so great after all.

This time I hadn't straightened up from my bow when somebody from the back called, "Engine Joe, Tomcat. Tell us Engine Joe."

"Ah, you don't want to hear Engine Joe," I retorted. "I've told you Engine Joe before. Have I told you The Pig?"

"Yes!" the crowd called in unison. "No Pig!"

"Engine Joe," somebody else called.

I put my hands in my pockets. Behind me, I heard Lindy clear her throat. I took my hands out of my pockets, smiled, and started to tell Engine Joe.

Sometimes the crowd loses interest in the story and asks for news from up and down the river. A flood at Cape Girardo, a dike washed out south of Cairo, the usual stuff. Sometimes I get sidetracked and tell about what we see from the *River Rat*. Like the time we nearly got frozen in for the season at Wildcat Landing. I remember snow geese in the marshes there, where the water steamed in the cold air like it was getting ready to boil. Sometimes I get started on a story and it changes as I tell it, so I can't remember afterward what I said. Sometimes the crowd just gets bored and dwindles back into a group of people sitting on the levee. But sometimes, the best times, the story has a life of its own and the crowd gets real quiet, and anyone who puts in a remark gets hushed up.

When I'd heard my third "hush," I decided Engine Joe was long but worth the trouble. I was well into the extended version, which calls for handstands on the deck rail. I was feeling pretty good. Scratched hands steady on the rail, keeping eye contact with the crowd even upside down, I'd just started to lift my left hand for my first step along the deck rail. And Esteban blew the whistle.

5

DEMOCRACY IN ACTION

ROM FAR AWAY, IF YOU LISTEN FROM shore, the *River Rat*'s steam whistle is strong and clear. It starts as a full-chested shriek of sound and un-ravels into separate tones only after an echo or two thins it out. From close quarters, if you listen from the main deck rail, it sounds as though the whole ship is alive and in pain.

I missed my left hand grip. I lost my balance, overcor-rected — and found myself looking down at the greasy water be-tween the hull of the *River Rat* and the stone wall of the levee. For a slow moment my right arm tried to flex enough to get back under my weight. I felt myself begin to topple. On half a breath, I clamped my mouth shut and tried to get ready to fall headfirst into the river. Rocks, I thought wildly. Then Lindy grabbed my ankle to steady me. I overcorrected again, and this time I really did fall headfirst, but only to the deck.

Lindy let my ankle go. "You okay?"

"Could be worse," I replied.

The crowd made a noise of disappointment as I scrambled to my feet. Not because the story was interrupted, either. So much for an encore. I drew myself up and gestured a reply to the boys in the back.

Esteban was halfway down the steps from the upper deck, the wooden bludgeon gleaming in his left hand. "Lesters coming," he called. He swung the club in a quick, wicked circle by its leather thong. "Think they want this back?"

Toby gave King a look that should have set him on fire and turned to help Jake with the mooring line. "Pilothouse, Esteban," she ordered. "Engine room, Spike. Stay there, you hear me? Lindy, put that chicken away and help Tomcat get the landing stage in. Get going!"

The crowd scattered back toward the gate of Bass City. Though sorry to miss any interesting fuss we might provide, they were unwilling to take part themselves.

Lindy and I swung the landing stage over as the mooring line came free. The current drifted us a little downriver. Then, somewhere in the *Rat*'s heart, her steam engine engaged the paddle wheel. Slow and steady, we began to move. Much too slow.

After Esteban, I was the next to see the Lesters. They came toward us in a pack, five burly red-faced men. They came around the Bass City wall from the old road along the river. For a split second, I thought they might have been running along that road ever since we left it in Fountains. I tried to pick out the hunter I'd left limping across the hillside. He wasn't there. But I saw hints of him in the pack, a family resemblance that had to do with thick necks and big arms and shirts too tight across the stomach.

They reached the riverside. Hot with the chase, the widening gap between us and the levee only seemed a small barrier as

68

the *River Rat* drifted out into the current. In unison they leapt for us.

Lindy and I were still at the rail. Astern, Jake and Toby were watching our pursuers. King was on the rail amidships.

Slowly the *River Rat* headed for the depths of the main channel. We were free of the Bass City levee and any reinforcements the Lesters might have with them. With Spike and Esteban running the *Rat*, there were four of us to handle the boarding party, provided King continued to stand around like a passenger. The *Rat* slackened what little speed she had. I hoped that meant Esteban had signaled Spike for dead slow and not that Spike was having trouble with the engines.

The Lester nearest me landed half across the deck rail. I pounced on him and tried to lever him over the side before he got his balance. One arm caught me under the chin hard enough to make my teeth snap shut painfully. His flailing hand clawed my shirt as I shoved him. Another push and I had him clean off balance. As he fell, his grip on my shirt nearly took me with him. I snaked out of his grasp and heard cloth tear. My best shirt.

As he splashed into the water, I turned to help Lindy. She was fighting a Lester with the name Duane on his shirt and needed my help about as much as ever — not at all. After a glance in her direction, I decided to let her finish up alone and turned to look for King. He was at the base of the steps to the upper deck. One of the Lesters had King's arm twisted behind his back.

"All right!" the Lester shouted, lifting the old guy's wrist at a cruel angle. "Everybody freeze or I'll rip his arm off."

No one paid any attention to the threat. Lindy had Duane squared off in front of her and was showing him a series of kicks,

69

chops, and blocks that left him staggering. Jake had sucker-punched his Lester before he got both feet on deck. The moment he rolled his guy overboard, he turned to help Toby with hers. She didn't need help any more than Lindy had. As her Lester moved toward her, she drew him in and past her, crooked a heel behind his knee to help him on, and sent him over the rail head-first.

King's Lester edged back onto the first step and raised his voice. "I *said*, everybody freeze!"

I looked from Toby and Jake to Lindy and Duane. Lindy was still showing her speed at his expense.

Toby put her hands into her pockets. "Lindy? You about done?"

Lindy paused, her back to the rail, and glanced at Toby in surprise. "Are you holding the curtain for me?"

Duane saw the opening he'd been hoping for and rushed at her. Lindy stepped aside. Duane shot past her and hit the water with a hefty splash. Lindy shook her head. "And I had so much more to teach him."

"Did you hear me?" King's Lester didn't sound like he thought we had. He backed another step up the stair as we turned toward them.

King's face had gone white at the pressure on his arm. The leverage forced him back against the Lester's barrel chest.

The Lester said, "Now, listen. You do what I say, got it? Or this guy's arm is coming out of its socket."

"Mere belligerence cannot compel obedience," said Esteban from directly behind him on the steps.

Startled, the Lester turned his head.

With great precision Esteban hit him just above his right ear. The Lester fell in a heap. King sprang away to stand against the deck rail. Esteban smiled around at all of us with great satisfaction, then said seriously, "Unforgivable to leave my post. I gave in to temptation." He went, cat-quick and cat-silent, back up the steps to the pilothouse.

Jake grasped the Lester by the collar and started to drag him aside. Lindy took the feet and helped lay him out where he would not block the steps.

"Lock him up," said Toby. She stepped close to King, studying him intently. "You all right?"

King nodded. "Good thing this happened after I played," he said, rubbing his twisted shoulder. "I don't feel much like using this arm now."

Toby put the tip of her right index finger into the middle of the old guy's chest. Her voice was very soft. "Feel like talking?"

King looked from her finger to her face. "Not right now."

In the silence that followed, I could hear the paddle wheel picking up speed. If any Lesters thought to swim after us, they had their work cut out for them.

"Too bad," said Toby, still softly. She jerked her head at the Lester on the deck. "Think *he'll* talk?"

King's eyes narrowed.

Toby nodded. "Right."

King swallowed visibly as he eyed the four of us.

As he hesitated, Jake hoisted the Lester up off the deck. "It's better to get their stories separately," Jake said. "I'll put this one away until we need him."

King said, "I'll tell you. But you won't believe me."

Toby smiled. "Talk."

King's attention was fixed on Toby. He knew by now that it was her reaction that mattered most. His voice was serious and nearly as soft as hers. "They're chasing me because they think I can tell them where something is. It's all a misunderstanding."

Toby looked skeptical.

"I was just passing through Rose Hill," King continued. "That's up on the bluffs west of Dresbach, where these guys come from. I stopped to ask for food. They wouldn't take music the way most people do. They made me work for it. At the end of the day I was full of dinner and feeling good, so I started to tell them a story. It's my favorite, about a man who finds a diamond as big as a hotel . . ." He hesitated. "Maybe you've heard it? No? Well, I guess it's really not important. Anyway, they misunderstood. They thought I was talking about something that really happened — that I was the guy who found the diamond. I told them — I tried to tell them — that if I was, I wouldn't be wandering around like this, now would I?"

Toby didn't bother to answer.

"But one of them said that if it were really as big as a hotel, I couldn't carry it with me," King went on smoothly. "And he said that since diamonds are the hardest thing there is, I couldn't break it into small pieces. But I must know where the diamond was. They wanted me to tell them."

At the look on Toby's face, Lindy and I moved to stand on either side of the old man. When she spoke, we traded a glance of alarm. Our first thought had been to flank the guy to keep him still. But the anger in Toby's voice made it seem like we might have to protect him from her.

"You fool," Toby said. She reached out to poke the old man's chest as she called him a fool. It was a pretty hard poke. "We might have lost the *River Rat* because of you." As she said "you," she poked him again. "We might have lost Tomcat. Esteban's hurt and it's your fault." When she said "your fault," I thought she was going to poke him again, or punch him. Maybe Toby thought so too, because she put her hands in her pockets. She glanced from me to Lindy. "Lock him up. Guard the door. When the Lester wakes up, we'll get the truth out of him."

King shook his head very slightly. "You don't buy the diamond?"

Toby looked from Lindy to King. Her eyes were hard.

The old guy shrugged and jerked his head in the direction Jake had taken the Lester. "You see what they're like. Not a nice family, no. The only virtue they have is persistence."

"Keep talking," said Toby.

"They think I can lead them to the riches of the Pharaoh," King continued. He glanced around to gauge our reactions. "You never heard of the Pharaoh? 'Open Season'? 'Danny Gets Back'? 'Loitering with Intent'?"

"Oh," said Lindy, "the Pharaoh."

"Oh, *that* Pharaoh," I said.

Right before the Flash, there was a musician, maybe you've heard of him, called the Pharaoh. He sold lots of discs, all about love and war and hairspray and the year 2000. He got almost all of it wrong, if you ask me. But "Loitering with Intent" is kind of a classic. Not too many words and a really evil bass line.

"The Pharaoh believed that the end of the world was on the way," said King. "He wanted a good seat for it. He could afford a real good seat. So he spent all his money building a vault to fill with all the things he'd need to survive. Food, clothing, music, toys — it was quite a place. I was there the day they installed the elevator."

"You knew the Pharaoh?" asked Lindy.

"I was in his backup band," King replied. "He invited us to come along. I declined the honor. But he wanted all our stuff on the computer so he could mix us if he needed us. I spent four days straight loading every lick I knew into his data base so I could be digitally remastered after the apocalypse."

"No wonder the old guy can play like that," I said.

"The Pharaoh's tomb," Toby said. "You know where it is. You said so to the Lesters. Not very bright."

King's lips parted in a curve, but it wasn't much of a smile. "Suicidal," he said. "The Lesters have a little country of their very own at Rose Hill. They run things to please themselves. I worked the harvest with them. There was a woman there."

Lindy grinned wickedly and said, *"Cherchez la femme."* I know what that means and how to spell it because I asked her later.

"To her I was just an old man. But I'd been places," King said. "Some of the places I told her about, she decided she wanted to go see for herself. You could hardly blame her for wanting to leave Rose Hill. She ran away one night. But you can't just up and leave a bunch like that, not when they need your muscles. And they feel . . . proprietary about their women."

Lindy snorted.

"They hunted her," King continued. "They brought her back. Because they had simple minds, they decided her problem must be simple too. Me. And so — " King broke off. His voice was perfectly level, his expression empty, but he wasn't looking at us anymore. He was looking past us, into his memory.

We let him look. Only the steady churn of the paddle wheel broke the silence.

King spoke again, measuring his words carefully. "They decided it would be simplest to kill us. If they had just gone ahead and done it, fine. I could have stood it if they'd done it quick." He hesitated. "But they decided we should dig our own graves. They walked us away from the buildings and showed us the place. A rocky patch, of course. You don't waste good crop land on something like a grave. They let us each have a shovel.

"You know, life isn't so great. Not life in Rose Hill, that's for sure. One day after another you scratch in the dirt, you try to get enough out of the ground to live through another winter. And why? So you can scratch again next year. All the time the sun burns you and the bugs bite you. It gets dark, so you have to stop working. Bigger bugs bite you. You sleep until it's light enough to get up and start all over. Things get bad, it's easy to think of reasons why you don't want to live. Funny thing, though. Things get really bad, all you think of is reasons not to die.

"There wasn't a spadeful of dirt I threw out of that grave that didn't have a reason to go with it. I knew I didn't want to die. More than that, I didn't want her to die. When the grave was waist deep, I put the shovel down and told them about the Pharaoh's tomb. I made them promise to let her go. And in return I promised to lead them to the vault and show them how to get in."

"I thought the Lesters didn't care for music," Lindy said.

King shook his head slightly. "I didn't tell them about the music. I told them about the generator. I told them about the supplies." He paused, met Toby's eyes directly. "I told them about the guns."

My jaw dropped. Toby took the old guy by the throat. Lindy said, "Guns?"

King watched Toby. His eyes were steady and a little tired. He said, "They like guns."

This is the way I learned it in school, back before the *Rat* went free: For a time right after the Flash, the one sure way to stay alive was to kill anyone who threatened you. Guns were very big in those days. But after a while, many of the people who wanted to stay alive so badly were dead just the same, victims of trying to stay alive at any cost. Most of the ammunition was exhausted, and the only weapons left were those that could be reloaded, like bows and arrows. What progress the survivors had made since was fragile. To rebuild on the wreckage of the Flash, after the disease and devastation that had followed it, took guts. If there was a single word that could strike fear into any survivor, it was *guns*.

If the Lesters would hunt so far up the river after a man who promised them guns, they would use the guns ruthlessly once they had them.

Toby released King. She studied him, frowning. "We can never prove you didn't tell us where the guns are. Even if we let you go, the Lesters will chase us instead."

"We'll have to let him go somewhere well out of their range," said Lindy. "If we give you a head start, you'll be all right," she told King. "They can't keep after you forever."

"They've been doing pretty good till now," I said. "How big a head start will it take? We're too far north already for this late in the year. Do you think you can lose them somewhere between here and Pig's Eye?"

Pig's Eye is the last mail stop we make. The river is navigable for a few miles farther north, as far as the rapids, but we don't go up there. We have no reason to, since no one lives that far up the river except the wild boys, and they don't get any mail. They don't barter, either. They run in packs and kill whatever doesn't kill them first. The only good thing about them is that they stay in the city. They have to.

The way I learned it, when people from outside see a wild boy, they take drastic measures. Maybe the wild boys lived with the pestilence that emptied the city because they were immune to it. But maybe they carry it, too. People don't take chances. Not healthy people. Not people who want to stay healthy.

Toby was still studying the old man. Her anger had given way to calculation. "If we come about, maybe the Lesters will keep heading north while we go south." Her mouth tightened as she dropped her gaze to the mail sack that lay, forgotten since the fight, beside the Lovich Chargeables. There were letters left in that sack addressed to landings north of us. If we came about and headed south, there would be no chance to deliver them until the river opened next spring. "There's enough moon to travel by tonight. But that means there's enough moon for them to see us by. We better take a vote."

King sneered. "Great. You order everybody around like a CEO until there's a real problem and then you call a committee meeting."

"Toby's our captain, not our commanding officer," Lindy retorted.

Jake came down the steps from the upper deck, his gray eyes hard and cold. "If you want to criticize Toby, we'll find a nice sandbar along here and set you down. You can take your pal along for company." He jerked his thumb back over his shoulder in the general direction of the Lester he'd locked away.

"Yeah," I said, "we'll just head south for a few years. It won't take the Lesters long to find you. Then they find the guns. We'll come back when the ammunition is all gone."

For a moment, Jake's expression froze into perfect blankness. Then he raised one eyebrow and said, "So you finally got him to talk. Guns?"

Toby turned from King to Jake. She didn't say anything. She didn't have to. Jake came to stand shoulder to shoulder with her. Without hesitation, without a single detail of the old guy's story, Jake was on Toby's side. And as usual, when standing beside her, he seemed to lend some of his strength to her.

Toby said, "It's time for that committee meeting." She looked back at King. "Unless you'd like to swim south without us?"

"I was swimming south without you when you interfered," King replied. "Remember what you said. The Lesters will never believe I haven't told you what I know. They'll hunt you instead."

"You're just saying that to make us feel better," Lindy said bitterly.

King grinned at her. "In fact, I'm just saying that because you told me I sure do know a lot of chords."

I'LL BE HONEST: I hate meetings. Nine times out of ten we all know what it is we have to do. The only question is when or how.

78

But we discuss the decision from every angle, consider the alternatives, and end up settling on the obvious choice after all. The tenth time out of ten, Esteban persuades us that there's no reason to make a decision at just that moment, and we adjourn. Of course, eventually there *is* a reason to make a decision and we have to call a meeting all over again — oh, it wears me out just to think about it.

I missed the first half of this meeting because I was able to persuade Spike that he should go hear King's complete story. Meanwhile, the boilers still needed someone to keep an eye peeled, so I volunteered to stand watch in the engine room while he went up to the pilothouse. This worked fine for about twenty minutes. Then Jake came down to the engine room.

"I've already told Toby that I'm voting with her," he said, taking the shovel out of my hand. "Why don't you go up and keep them in line while I see to things down here?"

"I'll come back and spell you in half an hour," I offered.

Jake tightened the left corner of his mouth, which means he's trying not to smile. "Come back when it's all over."

Struck by a sudden thought, I regarded him closely. "You don't like meetings any more than I do, do you?"

Jake started to shovel coal, so I couldn't see his expression. "Get on up there, Tomcat, or I'll ask Esteban to explain common law and constitutional government to you."

WHEN I GOT to the pilothouse, Spike and Lindy made room for me on the floor between them. I crossed my legs under me and listened. King's account was complete, and the debate on what to do with him was under way.

"I agree the Lesters won't believe we didn't make King tell us where the Pharaoh's guns are," Spike was saying, "so let's make him tell us."

King sneered. "How are you going to make me tell you, kid? Am I supposed to walk the plank?"

"Even if he wanted to tell us, and I don't think he does," Lindy said, running a hand through her hair to push it out of her eyes, "we don't want the guns."

"Oh, come on," Spike exclaimed. "That's like saying we don't want food and firewood."

"No, it isn't," Lindy replied. "It's like saying we don't want to be followed around by lunatics. Just think about it for one second, Spike. Suppose we had the guns, suppose we kept one step ahead of everyone who wanted to get the guns away from us — sooner or later, somebody would beat us, and then they'd have the guns and the *River Rat*, too. All I'm saying is, think about it for one second."

"Even if no one defeated us," Esteban said, without looking away from the river, "we might come to resemble that which we fear. And ultimately we would be the threat, possessed of the guns and the *River Rat*. Is it your ambition, Spike, to be feared?"

"But we're the good guys," Spike protested.

"Sure," said Lindy. "Now."

"Well, this is just about typical," I observed. "We're wasting time arguing about things while we ought to be doing something."

Lindy lifted her eyebrows. "I suppose you have the whole thing figured out?"

"Well, at least I know what the problem is," I said. "If we let the old guy go, do we let him go now? Or upstream? Or downstream?"

King released a long breath of exasperation. "You know, kid, I'm not that old. And I *did* tell you my name. Will you quit calling me the old guy?"

"Will you quit calling me kid?" I retorted.

"There's no reason we have to let him go, upstream or down," protested Lindy. "We can keep him with us. You heard him play. He can earn his way as a musician. We can swear him in as one of the crew."

"He's too old," said Spike. "Anyway, he wouldn't last a week. He won't eat oatmeal."

"Oatmeal is not part of our oath," Lindy reminded him.

"Tomcat's right," said Toby.

Silence fell in the pilothouse. Everyone but Esteban stared at Toby in astonishment. Even me. I am right lots of times, but nobody ever comes right out and says so.

"We're wasting time," she continued. "What's our position, Esteban?"

"We're nearly to Hendy Bend," Esteban replied. "We might make Pig's Eye if we put on the speed and get another clear evening. But there is weather coming from the east and I don't think we'll get our moon tonight. So say we tie up at Hendy, we can be in Pig's Eye by the middle of the morning tomorrow."

"If we drop you ashore when we tie up in Pig's Eye, do you think you'll have enough of a lead on the Lesters to be free of them for good?" Lindy asked the old guy.

King looked grave. "No, I don't think so. Maybe you should put me ashore right here."

"But then your lead is even less," said Lindy. She broke off at the look Esteban and Toby exchanged, a glance of suspicions confirmed. Lindy's brows shot up. "You don't want to go north," she said to King. "The farther north we go, the more you're worried the Lesters will catch you. So . . . where is this Pharaoh's tomb, anyway? Pig's Eye?"

King turned to Spike. "Get out that gangplank, kid. I'm not answering any more questions." He looked back at Lindy, serious again. "Don't revive that crew idea or I might surprise us both."

Lindy folded her arms. "Any other orders?"

"I saw that chicken you took on board," King said. "I like my eggs sunny."

"Eggs are Tomcat's department," said Lindy.

"What do eggs have to do with it?" demanded Spike. "Are we going to Pig's Eye?"

"That is the question," said Esteban. "Give us your counsel, Spike."

"We don't want the guns," Spike replied. "We don't want anyone else to get them. So we have to get King away from the Lesters. If we put him ashore now, the Lesters will catch him. If we wait until we get to Pig's Eye, he won't go ashore. So what are we going to Pig's Eye for? Let's just head south right now."

"We're already too far north for this late in the season," I added. "What if we get frozen in at Pig's Eye?"

"That's right," said Lindy. "If the river freezes, we'll have more to worry about than a bunch of Lesters."

"Do I get a vote?" asked King.

"I suppose you think this is funny," said Lindy. She turned to Esteban. "Tell King about common law and constitutional government, Esteban."

Esteban shook his head. "He doesn't know how much he

doesn't know. Such listeners make a poor audience. I vote with Spike."

"So do I," said Lindy. "So does Tomcat."

I turned to her. "What makes you so sure how I vote?"

"I know that look of yours," Lindy replied. "You only want to hold out until Toby and Jake vote. If they're with Spike, you'll make it unanimous. If they aren't, you'll do anything you can to keep from tying the vote."

I glared at Lindy but couldn't think of anything to say. She was just plain right.

"What happens when you get a tie?" King asked Lindy.

"We keep on arguing until someone changes his mind," Lindy replied. "Usually Jake or Tomcat. They both hate these meetings."

"Jake and I vote with Spike," said Toby. "Tomcat?"

I got to my feet. "Let's go south."

6

STAND BY
TO REPEL
BOARDERS

IT WAS LATE AFTERNOON AND I WAS TAKING my turn guarding the cabin door when Toby and Jake came to look at our Lester. He was awake. Halfway through my shift I'd heard him through the door, using the bucket we'd left him. Esteban says head injuries can take a person that way. When Toby and I unbarred the door, the Lester was sitting on the edge of the bunk, his head cradled in his hands.

He looked up slowly and asked, "What do you want?" He was trying to sound mean but it came out frightened instead.

"What do *you* want?" Toby countered.

The Lester looked confused. "I want to get out of this hole."

I frowned. His cabin was exactly like mine, a room maybe six by eight, with chalky green paint peeling off the walls and ceiling, and two bunks bolted to the wall like bookshelves. Only difference was, mine had a window, no bar on the door, and no bucket. "What's wrong with it?" I demanded.

"It stinks," the Lester said.

I glanced at the bucket but Toby gave me a look, so I kept quiet.

"We came to find out what you're doing aboard our ship," Jake said.

The Lester hunched his shoulders. "I don't have to tell you anything."

"True," said Toby.

Jake added, "Then again, we don't have to let you go, either."

The Lester looked up. "You're going to let me go?"

"Probably," said Toby.

"Why don't you make it easy on yourself and tell us why you and your friends have been chasing the old guy?" Jake asked.

The Lester eyed Toby, then Jake, then me, then looked back at Toby. "When are you going to let me go? Where are we?"

"It's not your turn to ask questions," said Jake. "Tell us about the old guy."

The Lester put his hands on his knees and stared at his knuckles. His voice was low. "He stole something that belongs to us. We want him to show us where he put it."

"What did he steal?" Toby asked. She leaned against the doorway, hands in her pockets.

"My cousin Becky and a brown mare about fifteen hands high," the Lester replied. "She was seven years old but still had no manners at all. Even so, we want her back. She's worth a lot to us."

"You're telling us that old man kidnapped a seven-year-old girl?" asked Jake. He sounded shocked.

The Lester looked up, surprised. "No, a seven-year-old mare," he replied. "Horse stealing is a hanging crime, you know."

"If he stole a horse," I replied, "it's funny he didn't use it to get away from you."

"I told you," the Lester replied, "he put her somewhere. He's got to show us where he put her."

Jake glanced at Toby. She frowned slightly. Jake said, "Your cousin and a horse. Anything else?"

The Lester shook his head. "No, sir. Nothing else."

Toby gave a small sigh. "I'm getting tired of questions." She turned to Jake and nodded.

Jake stepped over to the bunk and loomed over the Lester without touching him. "We know all about what really happened," he said. "Don't you think the old guy told us?"

The Lester swallowed. "What did he tell you?"

"It still isn't your turn to ask questions," Jake replied. "Maybe you just don't want to go home. Rose Hill doesn't sound like much to me. Maybe you should all run away."

The Lester looked down at his knuckles again. "So he did tell you. Well, all right. We made a deal with him and he broke his promise. We want to make him keep it."

"No matter what it takes?" asked Jake. "No matter who drowns?"

The Lester straightened up so suddenly he almost hit his head on the upper berth. "Just you remember that my pa is looking for it and my pa gets what he goes after. Remember that." The Lester smiled fiercely. "You can do what you want to me. My pa knows who you are, and when he's got it he'll get you."

"Threats?" inquired Toby. She looked at Jake and me, brows up. "What should we do with him?"

"Lock him up," said Jake.

"Keelhaul him," I suggested.

"Lindy's for making him walk the plank," Jake added.

Toby turned to the Lester. "We have to discuss this."

Jake said, "You don't mind if we lock you up again in the meantime, do you?"

Before the Lester could reply, we'd done so. The bar back in place, I leaned against the door and gave Toby and Jake my best pirate leer. "I've changed my mind," I said, my voice pitched to carry through the door. "I vote we make him walk the plank."

"Wait until we're back at Dresbach," Toby murmured. "We'll let him walk it there."

By sundown, or what would have been sundown if we'd been able to see the sun, it was raining hard. I came off guard duty to take soundings. It was completely dark. The heavy rain made the deck slippery. Beside me Lindy crouched under a fold of canvas, sheltering the galley lantern. The light it cast made her face and hands look golden, turned her pale hair amber, but it wasn't strong enough to reach past the rail into the darkness beyond. When I pulled the pole back from the first sounding and checked the depth in the lantern light, I had only the tug of the current to tell me that I was sounding the river. Otherwise it was like leaning out into nothing.

"Mark four," I said, and tightened my grip on the pole. It was cold and just damp enough to feel like it had been greased.

Lindy lifted her head to call back over her shoulder to Jake, "Mark four."

"Mark four," called Jake, above us on the upper deck.

It was a slow way to get the word to Esteban, but the wind could snatch a shout away to ears we didn't want to reach. The lantern was essential. Yelling was not. The chance that the foul weather would conceal our passage was worth a night run.

I took the next sounding. "Mark four." My shirt and jacket were damp through already and a line of rainwater had found its way down my collar. I gathered myself for the next sounding. If I worked hard enough and long enough, maybe I would get warm.

"Mark four," said Lindy.

Like a blind man sweeping the path ahead with his cane, the *River Rat* made its way downstream as I felt our way in the dark.

My back got sore. My arms got sore. The pole got heavy. The rain kept running into my eyes and mouth. I never did get warm.

On about the ninety-ninth sounding, I leaned close to check the pole in the lantern light. The wind was pushing me so hard that I had to crouch down against it. The lantern flickered crazily. I wanted to be sure about the level, but I had to blink and blink to see the markings on the pole.

"Quarter less twain," I mumbled finally. I straightened to take the next sounding. But I couldn't move the pole. I tried again to straighten and lost my grip on the pole completely. I doubled over, ready to fall on it before it rolled off the deck. But it wasn't on the deck. I stayed bent over, trying to blink my vision clear.

"I said, you can stop for a while," said Jake, measuring his words carefully, as if he had been arguing with me.

I put up my hand to wipe rain off my forehead and out of my eyes. Piece by piece, I put things together. Jake was holding the sounding pole. He had taken it away from me. I put my hands under my arms to warm them. My fingers felt brittle with cold, like frozen twigs.

"No point in letting you get so tired you fall overboard," said Jake. He lifted the pole and bent to make the next sounding. "Quarter less twain," he said.

"Quarter less twain," called King. He shrugged. "Whatever the hell that means."

I turned to look at Lindy. She was gone. In her place, King crouched under the canvas, sheltering the lantern. King read my puzzled look. "Lindy went to help shovel coal," he said. "She said she needed to warm up."

"You need to warm up, yourself," Jake said to me. "Go on. I'll take over here."

I didn't argue. I couldn't. My teeth were chattering too hard. I made my way to the engine room. It seemed like a long walk. The deck was almost icy. My back was so stiff I couldn't quite stand up straight. So I shuffled along, head down. I made it, mostly by reminding myself that behind the heavy door was warmth and light from the open firebox. Once inside, I slid down in the corner closest to the boiler, folded my arms across my knees, and watched stupidly as the rainwater ran off me to make little rivers in the coal dust.

Lindy looked up from her shoveling. She had a streak of coal dust smeared across one cheek. It looked like a bruise. "Well, finally," she said. She checked one of the gauges and then leaned on the shovel to inspect me.

"Great," said Spike. "A new recruit." He was sitting on my favorite upturned bucket, picking the shell off a hard-boiled egg.

Lindy and Spike stared at me. I stared back.

Before Spike joined us, Lindy was the one who spent the most time with the engines. She would have liked to give Spike the benefit of her experience, I think, but Spike had nine times more experience with steam engines than she did, so she couldn't. Oddly, Lindy didn't resent this half as much as Spike did. For months after he joined us, he blamed all kinds of silly problems on Lindy's management. It was nearly a year before he would let Lindy work in the engine room without him, even though she'd been doing it long before he ever laid eyes on the place. Now, as usual when the stakes were high, the River Rats had forgotten past disagreements. Spike ate his egg without paying the slightest attention to Lindy's occasional adjustment of the gauges. If I'd laid a hand on his precious levers, Spike would have made me stand in the corner. I wondered if Spike's former attitude toward Lindy would reappear someday when we had time for our usual arguing.

I realized Lindy was still staring at me. I'd been looking right at her without quite seeing her.

"Give him the shovel," Spike advised. "It's time you had a break."

"Let Tomcat alone," said Lindy. "He's had a rough night." She scraped up another shovelful of coal and grinned at me.

I gave her a crooked smile in return. It didn't begin to express how grateful I was, but I was too tired to think of anything to say. I put my head down on my folded arms and felt the warmth coming slowly back to my hands. It hurt, like putting my fingers into boiling water, but it didn't keep me awake.

I DON'T KNOW how long I slept. They say the bad nights take forever. It seemed like I'd been away for years. It was still dark when I went out to take the sounding pole back from Jake. King was still crouched down with the lantern. In the golden light I could see that Jake looked as miserable as I'd felt earlier. His hair was standing up in wet spikes, the collar of his coat was pulled to his ears, and he looked even wetter than the deck. When I took the pole away from him, he just stood there shivering.

I made the sounding. "No bottom," I called. Over my shoulder I said, "Spike had a hard-boiled egg a while ago. Why don't you go see if Lindy's chicken has laid another."

Jake squared his shoulders. "If it's Lindy's chicken, I'm not surprised it lays hard-boiled eggs."

I paused before the next sounding to take a closer look at him. "You can't be as tired as you look."

"Yes, I can." Jake turned away, squared his shoulders again, and started slowly up the steps to the upper deck. "No bottom," he called to the pilothouse.

I WAS STILL sounding when I detected the first sign that the night was finally coming to an end. Although the wind held steady, the rain had slackened, dwindling into a fine spatter, like mist. I took another sounding, and when I straightened my back the river seemed lighter, a ghost of the sky. If I narrowed my eyes, the riverbank on the right looked black against mere dark.

I kept sounding, calling off the depths, but all my attention was on the coming of the light.

The riverbank was directly to our right. I rose from a sounding that found no bottom and saw the curve of the bank, distinct against the dark, running across our bow a hundred yards ahead.

"Is Esteban asleep?" I called. "There's a point dead ahead."

"Point dead ahead." King repeated my words, alarm lifting his voice.

I bent low, desperate for the sounding. Still I found no bottom. Ahead I could see the obstacle more clearly. It wasn't a single point. It was three clumps of darkness, like the clumps of brush that grow on a sandbar.

"Hard to port!" I yelled. "What's the matter, you blind?" I knew Esteban couldn't hear me. I didn't care. We were going to rip our hull out on a sandbar and I'd have the best seat in the house to watch it happen.

"Soundings, Tomcat," Toby called down from the upper deck, her voice even. "Esteban wants soundings."

Obedient to the tone of command in her voice, I bent and straightened. "No bottom," I called. "Gee, Toby, can't *you* see it? By the time the bottom starts to shelve, we'll be too close!"

"No bottom," called Toby. Her voice was cool and clear, without any expression.

To the east the sky was green with the coming dawn. The current drew us on. By now the sandbar was so close I could make out branches against the gloom. In the darkness below the clumps of brush, I thought I could see foam caught in the weeds, like it had washed up on the sand. I doubled over the rail, still working the sounding pole with all my might. Blind or asleep or just plain crazy, Esteban was going to run us aground unless I found river bottom and made him change his mind.

Toby got tired of waiting for my sounding. She called down almost impatiently, "Tomcat?"

"No bottom," I called back through clenched teeth. "Are you going to wait until I can touch that sandbar with the pole?"

I looked ahead. The sandbar was square in our path, less than fifty yards ahead. Beneath my feet the vibration, as familiar to me as my own heartbeat, eased as the paddle wheel slackened its pace. Gradually, the *River Rat* altered her course to port.

I bent for another sounding, let out a long breath of relief. "Mark three," I called. "Welcome back, Esteban," I muttered to myself. "Cut that one pretty close, didn't you?"

"Sounding!" called Toby.

I bent again. "Quarter less twain," I called. "Shelving fast here."

Esteban cut the engines and swung us back to starboard.

"Hey!" I said, as the point swung back into our course. "Wrong way!"

With a thud we struck. My leg hit the rail and I bounced back, lost my footing, and hit the deck on my right elbow. As I got to my feet, I heard the engines go into full reverse. Only then I realized that we had struck on the port side, not the starboard. I moved along the rail to my left and probed with the sounding pole. Nine feet down I found the sandbar.

Ahead of us, twenty yards away, the clumps of brush were clearly visible, three tangles of tree branches bobbing on the current. Behind me King was leaning over the rail, watching the riverbank. All he said was "There they are," but the fear in his voice made me turn and stand close beside him, my sounding pole ready.

From the riverbank, with empty oil drums to buoy them, came the Lesters, roaring. Even in the half light, even in the first few moments, there was no way to mistake their numbers. The situation was plain. There were far too many of them. They were far too large. It was hopeless to resist.

From overhead, Toby's voice was cool and clear again. "Stand by," she called. "Stand by to repel boarders."

King's voice quavered a little as he said, "Well, I'll try. But I don't see how I can possibly repel them half as much as they repel me."

We tried to make it hard for the Lesters to get aboard. At first we succeeded pretty well. There was no victory in that, though. For we had to fight them on one level while they fought us on another. The Lesters were out to get aboard us any way they could. We had to fight the Lesters while we struggled with the *River Rat* herself.

When the trap was sprung, Esteban and Spike were in the pilothouse and engine room. For the first vital minutes of the fight, they were battling to back the *Rat* off the sandbar. Then, surrendering that notion, they were delayed by the mechanics of the *River Rat* and her engines. Before they could leave their stations, they had to halt the engines and secure the wheel.

By the time the *River Rat*'s paddle wheel was quiet, the fight was all but over. The Lesters were aboard in force. Lindy and I were back to back on the main deck. The combat zone she established with feet and fists was wider than the one I kept with jabs of the sounding pole. I couldn't see Jake or Toby, but I could hear them. I'd lost track of King.

From forward I heard the occasional dull sound of a blow landing, which I hoped meant Esteban and his bludgeon had arrived. Spike rushed out of the engine room toward Lindy and me. We hailed his arrival with as much joy as short breath allowed. I put my pole between a Lester's legs as Spike engaged him. The Lester went down as Spike yelled, "The doctor!"

Lindy left her place behind me and pounced to join Spike. The doctor was eight feet away. I lunged with my pole, fighting to guard their backs. If they reached the doctor in time, Spike

95

and Lindy could pump riverwater in to cool the boilers. If they didn't make it, the *River Rat* would surely leave the sandbar. But not in one piece.

The Lesters had the advantage of numbers but weren't very organized and weren't expecting any of us to charge them. When Lindy and Spike headed for the doctor, it took them a minute to figure out what was happening. Lindy and Spike dodged between a pair of Lesters who had tangled each other up in their eagerness to attack. Another pair intercepted them. One on one, they engaged Lindy and Spike, blow for blow and kick for kick.

"No time for this," said Spike through his teeth. He slipped aside and blocked Lindy's Lester. Two blows, and a Lester had Spike in his grasp. But that was one Lester too busy to stop Lindy. She sidled between two Lesters, dived, and hit the doctor with all her strength.

The hiss of steam escaping seemed very loud to me, even louder than my own breath rasping. As the Lesters converged on Lindy, I tried to get there first with the butt of my sounding pole. I got to give them just one solid blow. Somebody clutched the pit of his stomach and doubled up, trying to swear. I heard somebody else say, "Damn kids anyway." I still think that was a compliment. Using the pole like a lance, I lunged again. Somebody hit me.

Either I rocked or the *River Rat* did. I tried to go down relaxed. I meant to slap the deck and roll back to my feet. Instead my head hit the deck. The lights that snapped on in my skull stayed on a moment too long. By the time I pushed myself up on hands and knees, the fight was over. A large hand reached down and brought me to my feet.

Ranged along the deck, each in the grasp of one or more Lesters, were Lindy, Spike, Jake, Esteban, and Toby. I turned my head a little, as much as the large hand would allow. In the cold gray morning light I could see clumps of brush bobbing in the current just ahead of us. I could see the rafts the brush and branches were lashed to, even the poles and twine that held the whole thing together. It still looked a little like a sandbar, but not enough to run aground for.

I looked at Lindy. She was already breathing normally, standing relaxed and balanced, staring calmly out at the open river. Three Lesters held her at arm's length. One brief fight and she'd already taught them a lot about unarmed combat. Spike and Jake stood nearby, scowling at the clumps of brush on the current.

I twisted to look at Esteban. He didn't seem to notice the Lester holding him by his undamaged arm. He wasn't looking at the fake sandbar, either. His eyes were steady on some point in the distance, some horizon only he could see. I tried to get some comfort from the fact that Esteban had ignored every word I'd said except the soundings themselves. It didn't help much.

I looked at Toby. She was glaring at a Lester standing squarely in front of her, a squat old man with the name Lester embroidered on the pocket of his khaki shirt. His rolled-up sleeves showed big hairy forearms, with sparse hairs like the bristles on a hog's back.

"You in charge here, son?" he asked Toby.

At first I felt surprised that he and his chums hadn't noticed that Toby and Lindy were girls. They seemed like the type who would treat girls a lot differently from boys. I don't mean that nicely. But then I thought maybe to them we all looked alike. He probably only guessed Toby was our leader because he'd heard her deliver orders.

Lester put his face close to Toby's ear and spoke very loudly. "Where's the old man?"

Toby just glared.

"You speak English. I heard you. And you aren't deaf. We want the old man and we want Bud. We saw he made it on board. You didn't kick him over the side later, did you?"

Toby didn't answer.

Lester jerked his head. Every Lester who wasn't needed to hold us set about searching the *River Rat*. Toby went very still. The rest of us followed her lead. Motionless, silent, we waited, eyes on whatever internal horizon could hold us steady, and listened to them tear through the *River Rat*.

From the upper deck we listened to the noise of things breaking, the sound of wood splitting, and a yelp; then the Lesters returned. They brought the Lester we'd locked up and King, limp as a dishrag, between two other Lesters.

Toby took a long look at King. He was a sorry sight, a ragged old man unconscious in the hands of his two strapping captors. Toby looked as if she would have been happy to bite him in half. After a moment, she turned that same expression on Lester.

Lester looked back at her, his face still flushed with the effort he'd put into boarding the *River Rat*. "You boys made me a lot of trouble," he said. "You realize that, don't you?"

Toby just went on looking at him.

Lester lifted his hand. "I want to sit down," he said.

One of the younger Lesters brought him a bucket, turned it over, and set it down on the deck. Lester arranged himself as comfortably as the size of the bucket permitted, then gestured again. "Bring him here. Put him down."

The Lesters carried King over and dropped him on the deck as if he weighed no more than a bale of hay.

Lester prodded him with his toe. He wore combat boots with laces that looked gristly and tough, like something that had been alive once. It looked to me as if any touch of that boot would hurt plenty.

King squeezed his eyes tight shut.

"Get up, you old faker," said Lester. He nodded to the Lester beside him, the one who'd fetched the bucket. "Shake him up, Chuck."

Chuck reached down for King's shoulder and shook him hard.

"Ouch," said King. He opened his eyes and pushed himself up on his elbow. "This is just great," he said, glaring first at Lester, then at Toby.

Toby stared at King. "You could have fought," she said. "You could have run. I thought you did run. But all you did was hide." Her voice was icy with disgust. I'm glad Toby has never had to use that tone with me.

King seemed to forget his fear of the Lesters in his annoyance with Toby. "I was going to run. I was going to jump overboard and swim for shore while you fought them off. But first you didn't fight long enough." He hunched a shoulder in a half shrug. "And then I thought, I'm sick of running."

Toby just looked at him.

Lindy's voice was so soft I could hardly hear it. "Oh, you are, are you?"

King heard her, though. "I am," he said. "I was a fool to run in the first place. I should have known that all along. Guess I'll just have to go quietly." He gave Lester a long look. "Let's go."

For a moment Lester regarded King in silence. Then he put his hand over his mouth. From behind his fingers came a noise like a squeal of escaping air. His face got real red. He took his hand away, and the squeal turned into a high squeaky laugh. He doubled over, shivering and squeaking on his bucket, until little tears ran out of the corners of his tight-shut eyes and lost themselves on either side of his nose. "That's good," he said, when he had breath enough to talk. "Oh, that's very good."

While he laughed, the younger Lesters exchanged looks of concern and confusion. Toby looked disgusted. King looked annoyed. I'm sure I looked just as blank as the rest of the River Rats.

Lester knuckled his eyes and sighed. "So you're a fool to have run in the first place, are you?" he said to King. "You'll go quietly, will you?" He reached out and took King's chin between thumb and forefinger, nodded it up and down for him. "Yes, that's good." Without moving his eyes from King's face, without releasing King, Lester said, "Daryl?"

"Yes, sir?" replied the Lester holding Spike. "I'm right here, sir."

"Bring that boy here," said Lester.

Daryl brought Spike to stand at Lester's elbow. He had his right arm looped under Spike's and his hand flat on the back of Spike's neck. I couldn't see what his left hand was doing. It was near Spike's jaw on the side away from me. Wherever it was, the hold kept Spike helpless in his grasp.

Lester's attention was all on King. "See that kid? Don't look at me. This is no staring contest. Look at the kid." He moved King's chin so the old guy had to look at Spike. "Break once and you know you'll break again. Take a good look at that kid and understand this. You won't go quietly. You won't go anywhere. You are going to stay right here and tell me where the guns are. Or Daryl will break that kid's neck." He jerked his head toward Toby. "And then that kid's neck. And on up by size until they're all dead."

"And then?" King's voice was low. He was looking at Spike.

Lester turned King's face back to meet his eyes again. "Nothing then. Because it won't go that far. Daryl will do the first one, because you won't believe me until it happens. But then you'll tell me."

King's voice was still very soft. He sounded like he was trying to avoid waking someone. "And then?"

"Then I get the guns," said Lester, as though he were explaining something to a little kid. "You don't believe me, do you? I didn't think you would. Daryl?"

"I believe you," said King. He wasn't looking at anything but the deck. I could barely catch his words. "I'll show you where the guns are."

Slowly, Lester shook his head. "That's what you told me before. That's not good enough now. Tell me."

"I'll have to take you there and show you. I haven't been there since before the Flash," King protested. "It's bound to look different."

"Talk."

Daryl's arm tightened.

"All right, all right," said King as Spike stirred in Daryl's grasp. "I'll talk. For all the good it's going to do. You follow this river north. Take a left at the waterfall. Bear west a few miles until you get to a house on a hill—"

"Quit talking," said Lester.

With a shrug, King obeyed.

Lester stared at him hard for a moment, then said, "You're talking about Pig's Eye. There's pestilence up there."

"Gee, that's too bad," said King. His voice was nearly normal again.

Lester turned to Toby. "Get this thing going," he said. "Take me to his waterfall."

"No," said Toby.

"No?" repeated Lester. "What's that supposed to mean?" He turned back to King. "You explain it to them."

"You don't have to," Toby told King. "Sorry, but we're not part of this."

"Daryl thinks you are," said King apologetically.

Toby looked at Daryl. "Don't be silly." She made an effort to sound patient. "Killing us won't get you anywhere. It's not the first time we've had trouble, you know. There used to be a lot more of us."

In a way this was true: We've had plenty of trouble. And back when the *River Rat* was first cut free, we had a dozen orphans aboard. But nobody ever got their neck wrung.

Lester eyed Toby thoughtfully and said, "I suppose you can't take us to Pig's Eye while your boat is on this sandbar. My boys will haul you off and you can repay us by taking us north— how's that?"

Toby shook her head.

Lester's face began to redden. "You act like you've got choices. You don't. We're going north. You know why. We don't need you to get to Pig's Eye. We really don't need you to compete with us for the guns. So get to work and take us north."

"Why?" demanded Toby. "As soon as we get to Pig's Eye, you'll do whatever you want."

Lester smiled slyly at King. "Ah, but suppose I give you my word that we let you go free — how would that be?"

"Fabulous," I said out of the corner of my mouth. "That changes everything."

"Shut up," said Toby and Lester in unison.

I shut.

Lester leaned back as much as his bucket allowed and took a long look around at all of us. "Well, maybe we better just keep things simple. I see a lot of old wood here, lots of old paint. Nothing burns like old wood. Let's try this last offer. We haul you off this sandbar. You haul us to Pig's Eye. And we won't burn this boat down to the waterline."

Toby didn't move. She didn't look at any of us. She was facing Lester, but she looked past him as if he wasn't there at all. The silence stretched. All I could hear was the small sound the river made against the *River Rat*'s hull, a slapping, steady and soft. "All right," said Toby. She sounded tired.

Lester said, almost as softly as Toby, "Let them go."

"Pa, they'll kick our teeth in," Bud protested.

Lester silenced Bud with a quick gesture. "So they beat you in a fight, so what? What are you afraid of now I'm here?"

They let us go. Lindy turned to glare at the Lesters who had held her, but all they did was glare back.

Lester turned his attention to King. "You've been pretty reasonable about this so far. Don't wreck things by acting stupid now. Daryl, put him back where you found him."

"Can't, sir," Daryl replied. "We broke the door."

"Well, put him someplace else, then. And post a guard."

They locked up King but left the rest of us free to crew the *Rat*. By the time it was broad daylight, we were at our stations, trying to work too hard to think about the wrongness of having the Lesters aboard.

Spike, Lindy, and I took our places in the engine room. With all three of us shoveling coal, there wasn't room for guards. Bud watched us from the open door. Spike followed Esteban's signals but played with the switches and gauges more than usual. I decided Spike was trying to make his job look harder than it was to impress Bud and the rest of the Lesters.

"I don't know what all the excitement is about," said Lindy as she scraped up more coal for the firebox. "If we can't get off the sandbar today, we'll just wait until it rains. The river will rise and float us off."

"Or," I said, "we could let the Lesters use our shovels and get them to lower the river bottom. That would probably be faster."

Bud paid no attention.

WE DIDN'T HAVE to shovel the river bottom. We didn't even have to wait for the rain, which started again in the middle of the morning. By then, Esteban had succeeded in backing the *Rat* free of the sandbar. In short order, we were headed north.

If the Lesters thought of taking the *River Rat* from us for themselves, they did nothing about it. Instead they passed the time by breaking some windows, kicking some doors open, and messing up our stuff. None of us had anything of value beyond the *River Rat* itself and our musical instruments. The Lesters didn't know enough to realize what they were ignoring, so they didn't do any real damage. At the end of the second day came the only moment when I feared serious trouble.

"Who killed my chicken?" Lindy demanded. She had come to the galley and seen that dinner was chicken stew. With a snarl she took the ladle out of my hand and turned to the nearest Lester, Daryl. "That's my chicken you're eating, isn't it?"

Daryl tried hard to swallow so he could answer. While he struggled to do that and breathe at the same time, I reached cautiously around Lindy to take the ladle away. I was cautious because it's not safe to stand behind Lindy when she's mad. Of course, when she's mad, it isn't really safe to stand in front of her, either.

"Natural causes, Lindy. Honest," I said, "the chicken got sick."

"Sick?" Lindy tossed her head. She let me take the ladle back as she stared at Daryl. "That's what we get for hauling passengers. First one, then a dozen, and then bad luck to match. Well, enjoy your meal, Daryl. With the luck we've been having, with where we're going, pretty soon you'll be as sick as the chicken."

JAKE WINS
AN ARGUMENT

L ATE IN THE MORNING, JUST ABOUT THREE
days after Toby had saved the *River Rat* and all our
lives by giving in to Lester, we put in at Pig's Eye.
Lester didn't like it, but Toby insisted on making a mail drop.
When both letters were turned over, Lester stepped up to Toby.
"Get on with it, kid."

Toby had to tilt her head back to meet his eyes. She said,
"This is as far as we go."

Lester laughed. "Not hardly. The old man said to take a left
at the waterfall. Let's go to the waterfall."

"There isn't a waterfall there anymore," Toby replied. Her
voice was perfectly level, but anyone who knew her could tell she
was getting impatient. Toby doesn't like to have to explain things.
"It's nothing but rapids now. The river is wild these days. We
could tear the hull right out of her if we take the *Rat* too close to
the rapids."

"Let's try," said Lester.

"It isn't safe," Toby said. "There's the pestilence farther up.
And wild boys."

"If it's so dangerous, how do you know so much about it?" demanded Lester.

Toby nodded toward the shore. "You think these people don't know? We've been warned about this. And before this, we've listened."

"Let's not listen now," Lester replied. "Let's not talk either. Let's just go."

Toby stared at him, then shrugged and turned to me. "Cast off."

Toby left for the pilothouse to go over our course with Esteban. Lester went off to his favorite spot astern, where he could watch the *River Rat*'s paddle wheel. I had the landing stage in and the line coiled by the time the wheel engaged and Esteban brought us out into the current.

North of the landing at Pig's Eye, where a muddy little river joins it from the west, the river gets wide among reed beds. North of that the river narrows and flows through a channel of broken stone and shattered cement. That's where the city begins.

I stood at the deck rail and watched the riverbanks draw in. I'd never been north of Pig's Eye before, but I'd heard the same stories everyone else had.

Once the city was bigger than New Orleans. Except for the pestilence, it was almost unscathed by the Flash. If it weren't for the water, the city might have lasted. The people at Pig's Eye show all the signs of knowing how to run a good place. But the city took its water right out of the river. And you can't drink the river. When the water reserves ran out, the migration south began. And when the migration began, so did the riots. By the time the fires were out, the city was dead. Only Pig's Eye, where they have pure water from the old brewery wells, survived.

The *River Rat* reached the deep, narrow channel lined with broken stone. First there was a broad expanse of burnt wreckage, crisscrossed with empty streets. This was where the houses had been, row after row of houses. Some were burned during the pestilence. Some were burned during the riots. The rest went when the city was empty of everyone except wild boys. Wild boys like to burn things.

Next came the warehouses, great boxes of concrete open to the sky, ranked first on one side of the river, then the other. Young trees grew thick among them, their leaves gone golden with the turn of the season.

Then came the high bluffs on either side. Atop one I saw a shell of a house, one wall intact nearly to the third floor. From an upper window hung what looked like a white bathtub, dangling from its plumbing like a loose tooth.

We slid past on the narrow channel, the river beneath us reflecting the steel-colored sky. We rounded a bend and found ourselves approaching the white water at the foot of the rapids.

Esteban put me to work sounding. With maddening slowness he brought us to a safe landing on the western bank. The paddle wheel stopped, the doctor let the pressure go, the engines rested, and we were silent at last, moored in the heart of the city.

Our view was hidden by the fallen walls and broken towers on either riverbank. Here and there, bare rock and raw earth showed the scars where a landslide had taken some of the shore into the river. Elsewhere the banks were slopes of gravel, treacherous footing up to solid ground. On the eastern bank I could see dull metal and concrete where rows of cylindrical storage buildings, some rubble, some almost undamaged, stood in an orderly rank. To our left, on the western bank, broken buildings ran north as far as we could see. If a wall held an empty window, treetops were visible beyond. Trees were everywhere. Once I thought I saw branches sway. Yellow leaves shifted for a moment and then went still. There was no wind. The only sound was the rush of the rapids, boiling white water that marked the end of the river for the boat.

One by one, the River Rats joined me at the deck rail, gazing upstream at the rapids. One by one, the Lesters came down and took up positions all around the *Rat*'s main deck. I wondered how long Lester had to coach them to do that right.

At last Lester came, with Bud and Daryl behind him holding King. He stopped at Toby's side. "Call this a waterfall?"

Toby folded her arms. "You want to go farther, you can walk."

Lester turned to King. "What was it you said, old man? Left at the waterfall?"

King shrugged as well as Bud and Daryl's grasp let him. "More or less."

Lester's little eyes danced. "What comes after that?"

"It's been a long time," said King. "Things have changed. I guess I'll have to show you."

"Things have changed, all right," said Lester. He jerked his hand toward Toby. "Show the kid and his friends. The boys and I will wait here for you."

Everyone protested.

Lester jerked his hand again. "I want those guns. I don't want to get sick. I'm staying here. If you decide you need the guns more than I do, you can keep them. I'll take this boat instead."

"But Pa —," Bud began.

Lester stopped him with a look. "You still afraid of these kids?"

"Pa, what if they use the guns to get the boat back?" Bud persisted.

"You worry too much, Bud," said Lester. "Why don't you go along with them to be sure they don't get sneaky? And just to even things up, I'll keep one of them with us. That way, if they try to use the guns on us, we can make that kid pay for their sneakiness."

Everyone objected loudly.

"I don't care who it is," said Lester, "but one of you stays. The rest go with him." He jerked his thumb at King.

"You can't run the *River Rat*," said Toby.

"We'll get the hang of it," Lester replied. "How hard can it be? You can do it, and you're just a bunch of kids. But I tell you what. I'll give you five days to get back here before I try. How's that for fair?" Lester loomed over Toby. "Five days before we untie that rope and leave you here. By that time, maybe the kid who stays behind will have taught us something about boats."

"Ten days," said Toby, "and you don't mess with the *River Rat*."

"One week," said Lester. "You have my word. But if you're late, we do what we please to this tub. If we can't run it, we'll burn it. And we'll burn our hostage, too."

"Seven days," agreed Toby, "but I'm the one who stays to make sure you don't forget you gave your word."

"Not so fast," said Jake. Toby turned to him as the rest of us circled her at the deck rail. For the moment the Lesters let us alone. Only Lester himself stayed in earshot. "Who says you're the one to stay?" Jake demanded.

"It's my responsibility," Toby replied.

Jake grimaced. "So much for constitutional government, huh?"

"Is this another committee meeting?" I demanded.

"How could we vote on this?" Spike muttered to Lindy. Lindy just glared at all of us.

"It's my place to stay," Toby said to Jake, soft but fierce.

Jake stood braced with his shoulders hunched a little, as if it took him some effort to keep still. He sounded reasonable enough, but though his voice was low and steady, it wasn't quite calm. "King has to go. Because of the *River Rat*, Esteban and Spike have to go. Either of them would be as good as a slave because of what they know about the engines. You and Lindy have to go. You know why. So that leaves Tomcat and me. So I have to stay."

I thought about arguing. Then I took another look around at the Lesters and decided I didn't want to. Whoever got left behind would have plenty to worry about and no control over any of it. And maybe, just maybe, at the end of the seven days, he or she would have to find a way to stop the Lesters from stealing or burning the *River Rat*. It was a tough assignment. I decided to keep quiet.

Toby's voice was sad. "I'm the captain. I have to stay."

"You're the only one who can begin to keep King in line," Jake countered. "You've got to go."

Toby said, "We'll vote."

"It's foolish for any of us to leave," said Esteban. "You should both stay. And so should the rest of us."

"That's not a choice we have," said Toby.

"Going ashore won't exactly be a walk in the park either," Lindy said. "If things are really that bad, what difference does it make where . . . where it happens?"

"It's six of one, half a dozen of the other," agreed Spike.

"If it's that bad," I said, "I agree with Esteban. We ought to stick together."

"Who says it's that bad?" Lindy demanded. "Do you think you can cut a better deal?"

I lifted my hands. "I never said so. But if things go wrong —"

Jake laughed softly. We quit arguing and looked at him in surprise. He made a gesture that included us all. "We're six of one and half a dozen of the other," he said. "This is something that can't be put to a vote. I volunteer. If things go wrong and it comes down to breaking necks, I've got the stiffest one."

"You've got that right," said Toby with a little puff of annoyance. "Well, things won't go wrong, that's all." She stood close to Jake, took the worn lapel of his coat in her hand, and tugged it a little as she said, "It's only a week. Maybe not that long. When I get back —" She broke off and looked at the deck.

"Yeah," said Jake and smiled a little. "When you get back."

"It's only a week," called Lester, still seated on his bucket. "Don't be late."

We all glared at Lester.

King let out a long sigh. "I'm ready when you are. But I don't leave until I get something to eat. And no oatmeal, either."

It took time to put together enough supplies to last us all seven days. The apples from Bass City helped. We left little aboard for the Lesters to eat in our absence, but if things got really desperate, there was always the oatmeal. With a blanket and a water flask each, by noon we were as ready as the resources of the *River Rat* could make us.

Jake watched us ashore and drew the landing stage back when we were safe on dry ground. At our mooring, shattered stone and concrete lay in a drift, sculpted by the river like a snowbank by the wind. Toby led us up the slope of gravel and broken rock. At the top of the bank we paused to look back at Jake.

It felt wrong to be walking away from the *River Rat*. From stem to stern we could see Lesters. With no more activity than their lazy guard duty, no smoke from the *Rat*'s stacks, the steamboat seemed lifeless, a wooden hulk tethered to the shore.

From the deck rail, his fists deep in the pockets of his ragged coat, Jake watched us. His face was expressionless.

At the top of the riverbank, Bud put up his hand to wave good-bye. No one waved back at him. When Toby led us inland, Bud shrugged and turned to follow. No one said anything.

Toby and King were in the lead. Lindy and Spike fell in behind me. Bud brought up the rear. Together we set out to search for the Pharaoh's tomb.

BEFORE WE'D GONE five hundred yards from the riverbank, all scent and sound of the river was left behind us. After the first slope the land leveled off. It was hard to get a sense of the terrain, though. The streets were twice as wide as the streets of Fountains, but they were lined with buildings. Everywhere I looked there were walls. I couldn't see the horizon in any direction. I had thought we could see a lot of buildings from the river. Now I realized we were headed straight into the thick of the biggest buildings I'd ever seen. Pretty soon we wouldn't even be able to see the sky, I thought, let alone the horizon. I quickened my pace to keep close to the others.

We picked our way down the center of the silent streets. Everywhere the pavement was cratered with time and weather. It had rained recently. Broad puddles reflected the iron gray sky and the lifeless chaos around us. The crumbled surface of the street was full of holes. Some of the holes were obviously man-made, deep shafts designed to go beneath the streets. With their metal lids in place, the holes looked like part of the surface. Some of them were missing their lids, revealing pipes or cables or the rungs of a ladder punched into the shaft's wall like giant staples. I wondered what was under the streets that had needed so much equipment to keep it going.

The streets we followed led us southwest. Most of the buildings we passed lacked roofs, some entire upper stories. It seemed that the taller the buildings were, the more punishment they'd taken. Most of them showed signs of fire long past. A few were connected at the second level with metal bridges, folded and twisted into a litter of steel and glass shards. Where walls had shattered completely, there were still cables left, metal rods that had once reinforced something. Now they just raked out of the rubble, tangles of wire and snares of steel.

Every window was open to the weather. The people in Pig's Eye say the wild boys like the sound of breaking glass. There were a few signs still hanging at crazy angles above the street. One read: Refuse Imitations. Why would anybody buy imitation refuse?

I was the first to open my ration of food. Munching one of the Bass City apples made me feel more cheerful as I picked my way through the intersections of wrecked wall and ruined street.

As I finished the apple, I noticed another open shaft ahead. Toby and the others passed it without a second glance, but I stopped to peer into the hole. I craned my neck but couldn't see the bottom. Metal rungs vanished into the darkness below. How far down did it go? I wondered. I dropped the apple core and listened.

"Tomcat," Toby called, "get a move on."

If the apple core made a noise, I missed it. Reluctantly I gave up the idea of investigating the metal rungs and hurried to join King and Toby and the rest.

"Are we almost there?" I asked, when I caught up.

King snarled at me and didn't answer.

Toby said, "We just started."

"Well, how much farther do we have to go?"

"Hundreds and hundreds of miles," King told me.

I looked at King. He would have been cross with me no matter what, but I thought there was more anger in his voice than even the annoyance of my presence could account for. "You do *know*, don't you?" I asked.

King snarled again.

"*Don't* you?"

Toby sighed. "Shut up, Tomcat."

BY THE TIME we crossed the heart of the city, it was beginning to get dark. King led us on across railroad tracks branching and crossing in all directions. Beyond the rail yard we found a snarl of roads and bridges like a knot of concrete and steel. Under the bridges lay a forest of concrete pillars, some smooth cylinders, some broken away to reveal cables at the core. Under a bridge King halted.

"We can stop here for the night," he said. "At least we'll be out of the wind."

"There isn't any wind," said Lindy.

"We have another hour at least before it's really too dark to travel," Spike added.

"It's really too dark to travel right now," King replied.

"I can see fine," said Lindy. "Can't you?"

"No, I can't," King said. "I'm too old to see. I'm too old to walk another step. And most of all I'm too old to argue. You don't want to stay here, don't stay. It makes no difference to me whatsoever."

"It's a difficult spot to defend," said Esteban.

"Do you think the wild boys know we're here?" asked Bud.

Spike said, "If they can't smell us, they aren't as wild as people make out."

"If the wild boys attack us," I said, "we're better off running than fighting, anyway."

Lindy grinned wickedly at me. "The way you fight, that's a fact." The grin removed some of the sting from her words. Not all of it, though.

"How much farther till we get to the guns?" asked Bud.

King sat down with a sigh of exasperation. "You too? I was in a car the last time I came this way. The drive didn't seem very far then. It's at the edge of a lake. Does that help you out any?"

"Which direction is the lake from here?" asked Esteban.

King sighed again. "West. More or less."

"Well, if Esteban thinks this place is hard to defend, I don't think we should spend the night here," said Spike. He turned to Lindy. "What do you think?"

"If you kids take another vote," said King very evenly, "I am going to scream." He pulled off one of his shoes. "You do what you want. I'm staying here."

Bud took up a post with his back to the nearest pillar and tried to look vigilant. "I'm staying with the old man."

"We better patrol the area before we settle in for the night," said Lindy.

Toby asked, "Any volunteers?" She glanced from Esteban to me. I can take a hint.

Toby, Esteban, and I had first watch. We left Lindy and Spike with Bud and King. King was rubbing his feet and muttering. Bud just sat beside him, about as much use as ever. Lindy and Spike were doing the actual work of setting up camp.

After a careful stroll around the area, we took places that gave us the best view out beyond the cylinders. I had a spot about a hundred yards from King, back toward the city, where I could lean against an outer pillar and strain my eyes into the darkness ahead, while I strained my ears to listen to the darkness behind.

There was nothing to see. There was nothing to hear. I leaned against my cylinder and thought about apples, and small game, and the possibility of finding something to eat in the city. Then, for variety, I thought about the pestilence. It's a nasty disease. It starts with a headache, goes to a fever, then to a bloody flux, and ends in a coma. Nobody knows why some people catch it and some people don't, but food and water supplies are as good a place to start as any. I decided I wouldn't like to catch the pestilence, from a wild boy or from anything else. I went back to thinking about apples and wished I hadn't been so quick to start on my share of the Bass City supply.

All this time, just to have something to do, I scanned the darkness from left to right every few moments to give the impression I was really guarding something from somebody. After about the hundredth scan I noticed a light off to my left. I couldn't tell what it was. It was too small for a campfire. It was too big for a candle. It was on the ground. And it hadn't been there a few seconds before. I stared. It didn't move. It just glowed steadily, shining like a beacon in the dark.

I watched it hard while I counted to one hundred. I couldn't hear anything. I couldn't smell anything. Very slowly, very softly, I slid back behind my cylinder and moved toward the light, keeping a row of pillars in front of me. It seemed like a good idea at the time.

The light was six pillars away, maybe fifty yards. When I peered around the closest cylinder there was nothing there but the light. Very slowly I came to get a closer look. It was a piece of wood about the size of my fist, charred black as though it had been pulled from a fire. Someone had poured something oily over it, maybe to make it burn better. The oil smelled like rancid meat. As I examined it, the oil flame began to flicker and die. The charred embers still burned but gave little light. Instead the fire shrank down into a dull red glow that crept inside the blistered, blackened wood. I scuffed dirt and gravel over it and drew back behind my pillar again. I listened hard. Nothing. Not even a breath of wind.

I started back to my post as silently as I could. When I came around the cylinder to my original spot, there was a shallow hole scraped at the place where I'd been standing watch. In the hollow burned a piece of charred wood about the size of my fist. I pulled back into the shelter of my pillar. Looking in King's direction, I could see a gleam of light. It flickered as though it were a small fire set in a hole scraped into the dirt. I set out for the light.

Moving fast in the dark is easy. Moving fast in the dark without making noise is hard. I did fairly well. Once I hit a pillar with my shoulder, but I glanced off and kept my course. Once I tripped over broken concrete and fell full length. The concrete crunched beneath me, and my clothes rustled as I got up, but I didn't say a word.

When I was close enough to the light to see and hear, close enough to be seen and heard if I wasn't careful, I circled. I was close enough to smell the fire, the same rancid oily smell. But I couldn't see anyone. I couldn't hear anyone. I stood listening until I could almost hear the hair on the back of my neck bristle. Nothing.

Then, the scrape of a footstep, and I came on guard as Esteban and Toby appeared at the far edge of the ring of firelight. I moved out of the shadow of my pillar so they could see me.

Toby lifted a hand to me, then gestured back the way I'd come. I shook my head. Toby glanced at Esteban. He wasn't paying attention to us. He stood with his head cocked, listening intently. After a moment he met Toby's eyes. She followed his look when he turned to stare into the blackness to the west. Then I caught it too — right at the edge of my hearing: the sound of a blow landing on flesh, and a stifled cry of pain.

Toby motioned me back and signaled toward the sound. I nodded. She and Esteban melted into the dark.

After a few paces I could hear better. There were two sets of hard breathing. I heard another blow land. When I could catch the sound of feet shuffling, I paused. I heard nothing from the direction Esteban and Toby ought to be coming from.

Another blow from the fighters, then an unmistakable sound — somebody's head hit something hard. A pillar? There was a scrape of cloth on a hard surface. Somebody sliding down a pillar into a heap on the ground? Two hard gasps for breath and footsteps were running toward me in the dark.

I stepped forward into the fighting stance I'd learned from Lindy. The runner hit me, and we went down in a tangle. Hands countered my grip the only way it could be broken, and I felt fingers hard on my neck. I slapped my hands into position and felt the fingers slacken.

"Tomcat?" whispered Lindy.

I managed a grunt, and the grip was gone. For a moment Lindy and I lay together in the dark, hearts hammering.

"Did I hurt you?" she asked, her breath warm in my ear.

"You wore me out," I assured her. When I started to move, a lock of her hair fell into my face. It tickled a little but smelled good. I stopped moving. "Are you all right?" I asked. "What's going on?"

Lindy gave me a hand up. I didn't need it, but I took it anyway. "One minute King was complaining about the dried beef," she murmured, "and the next we were buried in wild boys. They're little but they're fast. One wanted to play tag with me. He got tired and fell down, though."

Our voices were soft, but Toby and Esteban found us in time to hear Lindy's reply to my question.

"Where are the others?" Lindy asked.

"Gone," Esteban replied.

"Blast," said Lindy. "How did they get past you?"

"They didn't," Toby said.

"I heard nothing," said Esteban.

It was embarrassing. I felt my ears get hot. I'd abandoned my post and gone off after a pretty light the way a kid chases a firefly. I let my breath go and said, "I didn't hear anything, but I saw one of their little fires and went to take a closer look."

Lindy sighed. "Oh, Tomcat!"

"Would you have done differently?" asked Esteban gently.

"*Yes*," said Lindy.

"We don't have time for this," said Toby. "Where's the one you fought?"

"He's still around here somewhere," said Lindy. She led us back to the place where she'd had her scuffle. By touch we found the wild boy, sprawled on the ground with a bump on his skull to show he'd met her.

By the time we got him back to our camp, the fire had faded to a dull red glow of embers. In the dim light we inspected him.

He was only an inch or two taller than Spike and much skinnier. His head had been shaved recently. The pale scalp was marked here and there with insect bites. His feet were bare — judging by his soles, they always had been. His shirt might have been red cotton once. Now it was mostly liver-colored ribbons of soiled cloth. To the belt loops on his pants he had tied three small pouches. Lindy undid them deftly. The first held a lump of charred wood about the size of a fist. The second held tinder, flint, and steel. The third, the smallest, was stuffed with long black hair.

"Yuck," said Lindy and scrubbed her fingers on her pants. The wild boy stirred.

We were clustered around him, Toby closest of all. She put her hands on his shoulders as he opened pale eyes and blinked up at her.

For a moment he held perfectly still. His eyes flickered back and forth as he examined us all. As he looked at us, his mouth thinned into a hard line. Then he looked past us into the dark, fierce yearning in his eyes. Whether or not he was listening for his wild boy friends, there was nothing. Then the yearning was gone and he looked even younger than Spike. He turned in Toby's grip and tried to get up.

Lindy grabbed one arm. I got the other.

He sank back against the pillar, Toby's grip sure on his shoulders. Then, so fast and so hard his teeth clicked together, he tried to snap at Toby's wrist. Esteban reached out with his bludgeon and rested the tip against the wild boy's chest to remind him he was outnumbered. The wild boy went still and stared at Esteban.

Esteban stared back. Even in the small glow the fire gave, his dark eyes held light. "They left you," he said, very soft, very gentle. "They went home and left you all alone. Do you want to go home?"

The wild boy didn't seem to understand the words, but he didn't take his pale eyes from Esteban's.

"You can go home," said Esteban, continuing in the same soothing tone. "That would be all right with us. You wait here until the fire burns out. Then we'll go home. Just watch the fire and listen to me. No, don't look at me. Just look at the fire and listen to my voice."

The wild boy looked at the fire. Esteban leaned closer, his words only a shade louder than a breath or a heartbeat.

"Watch the fire burn and then we'll go home," said Esteban.

The wild boy watched the fire. His chest rose and fell in rhythm with Esteban's soft slow words.

"The fire is burning low," said Esteban. "It's nearly out."

I didn't move my head, for fear I would scare the wild boy. But I shifted my eyes to look at the fire. It was smoldering but it wasn't out yet. I looked back at the wild boy. His blue eyes were empty.

"The fire is out now," said Esteban. "Time to go home." He lowered the bludgeon, and Toby released her grip on the wild boy's shoulders.

For a moment he sat there, just staring into the fire. Then, though his eyes were still empty, he got to his feet. His first steps were unsteady, like he was dizzy from standing up too fast. He walked east, back toward the heart of the city. As silently as we could, we walked beside him in the dark. All of us followed Esteban's voice as the wild boy led us home.

8

WILD BOYS

BY THE TIME WE FINISHED WALKING across the railroad tracks, I was all ready for a re-match with the wild boys. Our guide seemed to have no trouble finding his way in the dark. He didn't even stub his bare toes on the railroad ties. Esteban, too, made his way easily. Just as well he did, for a fall on his broken arm would have been bad. But the rest of us tripped regularly. Even when we were able to keep from making any noise in words (and I thought of some good words), our breathing was full of sudden gasps and hisses of pain.

After the railroad tracks came the cluttered streets again. Even in the dark I could feel the way the buildings blocked the horizon. I hated those streets. The dead city felt all wrong to me, empty and crowded at the same time. I tried to move as quietly as I could, but within about ten minutes, I'd managed to step in puddles with each foot. After that I moved with a mushy noise at every stride.

Our wild boy ignored the gasps and squelches. He didn't seem to notice that anyone was with him. All the way, Esteban's voice, strong and soft, full of assurance, soothed him. When the wild boy left the center of the street to pick his way across a drift of rubbish to one of the buildings, we, too, found ourselves drawing assurance from Esteban's voice.

When the wild boy led us up a ramp to a cold metal door, we paused. I felt Lindy's hand brush mine.

"What are we doing?" she whispered in my ear. "Are we just going to walk in?"

Our guide fumbled a moment at the left side of the door, then banged on the metal panel with what sounded like a piece of chain. The noise made us all jump.

"We are on a path," said Esteban. "Each breath brings us a step along the path. There is no turning from the way."

"Just what is *that* supposed to mean?" demanded Lindy in a fierce whisper.

"They've got Spike," said Toby in a tone that ended the argument before it began.

Esteban said, "While the wild boys have Bud and King, we have no way to free Jake. So we have no choice. We must confront them."

"Right *now?*" murmured Lindy, but her words were so close to a breath that I think only I heard them.

A gust of warm air, smelling of scorched feathers, met us as the door swung outward. Within, the floor and ceiling of a huge torchlit chamber slanted upward, climbing gradually into shadow. Our wild boy stepped across the threshold.

"Now," said Toby.

So we followed our wild boy home.

Ten steps inside the chamber was the metal skeleton of a glass-walled booth, the glass completely gone. Inside the booth sat a wild boy, a small pink-cheeked one, leaning his chair back on its legs. Beside the booth was a red metal crossbar jutting out into our path. Overhead was a sign, black lettering on a white board. It read: Clearance Seven Feet. Stop and Take Ticket.

As we followed our wild boy past the crossbar, the sentinel brought his chair back to the floor with a clatter.

"Hey, good going, Wilson!" he called. "You got 'em."

Lindy and I exchanged looks. Our faith in Esteban was great, but it wasn't perfect.

Wilson paid no attention to the pink-cheeked boy. He walked on like he didn't see or hear anything.

"We didn't start the party yet," said the pink-cheeked wild boy, leaving his booth to come with us. "Just in case you got the rest of them."

Wilson kept walking.

As we went up the sloping entryway with him, I looked around. The walls were lined with salvaged wood of every kind. Panels and planks leaned at crazy angles, scrawled over with painted symbols and illegible words. Here and there, drafts of cold air made me wonder if there was anything beyond the makeshift walls but the night outside.

At the far end of the chamber, Wilson led us around a corner and up into another chamber, as big as the first. There were more torches, along with some tin can lamps burning oil that gave off a smoky yellow light and a rancid smell. The light got better as we continued upward.

We followed Wilson up two more levels before we came to the rest of the wild boys in another big room, this one lined with paper, from rain-blistered posters to brown pages from paperback books. In the center of the chamber burned a fire, a restrained one, more for cooking than for entertainment. I looked at the spit over it. From the shape of the meat on the spit and the smell of singed feathers, I guessed they were having pigeon for dinner. The bones were the wrong shape for rat. From the color I judged the pigeons were just about done. Also on the skewers were wild onions and knobby little potatoes. Except for the feathers it all smelled pretty good. I wondered if wild boy food would give me the pestilence.

Around the fire were more wild boys than I'd ever wanted to see in one place. Many of them were no bigger than Wilson. Some had close-shaven heads like his, but most had manes of tangled hair as long as mine, worked here and there into braids. All wore rags. None wore shoes.

As Wilson led us in, all activity around the fire ceased. Every face turned to us. Even the boy turning the spit stopped to inspect us. We looked at them and they looked at us.

Into the watchful silence the pink-cheeked wild boy said, "Well? Where is everybody?"

Lindy and I traded looks. It seemed like there were plenty of people there already.

The wild boy at the spit said, "Red took them upstairs."

Pink Cheeks turned to us. "Come on. We don't want them to start without you."

I wasn't so sure about that, but Wilson led us across the room to another passage, this one curtained with ragged canvas to keep the cold air out. Past the curtain was another ramp that led up and out onto the roof. There we found a crowd of wild boys bearing torches. With them were Spike, King, and Bud.

At the sight of our companions Toby moved forward. The crowd of wild boys parted before us to reveal a white-haired wild boy with a white scarf knotted about his throat. He moved forward to stand between Toby and our companions. The cold breeze lifted the long fringes of his scarf and stirred its strangely knotted border. In every other way his rags were the same as the others', but there was no doubt he was their leader.

"Red!" cried Pink Cheeks. "Wilson came home."

"I can see that, Zeke," said the white-haired wild boy. "Don't worry. We wouldn't start without him." He looked at Toby. He didn't seem to have any doubt who our leader was.

Toby and Red eyed each other as Lindy and I flanked Toby and Wilson. Esteban halted behind us.

"You all right, Spike?" Toby asked, without taking her eyes off Red.

Spike stood in the heart of the crowd of wild boys, Bud and King on either side. At the sight of us he squared his shoulders. His voice was crisp and steady. "We're fine. You?"

"We're fine," said Toby. When she spoke to Red, her tone was very different from the one she usually used. Instead of getting by with as few words as possible, she sounded almost chatty. She spaced her words as if she was talking to a little kid, very slow and gentle. "What are you doing out here in the cold? Waiting for the northern lights? It's too cloudy tonight."

"We were showing your friends our clubhouse," said Red. He smiled at Toby. I realized that he had a nice face, for a wild boy. His teeth were almost all there and his eyes were clear, so dark they seemed black in the torchlight. "See for yourself."

He gestured, and the crowd of wild boys drew back a little so we were able to see beyond him. The roof was flat, surrounded by a low wall. In the northeast corner a ramp led down and away from the building. It was hard to be sure in the torchlight, but it seemed to curve tightly back as it descended, as if the whole building was moored to a spiral of concrete.

Lashed to the head of the ramp with ropes and cables was a car. I don't know much about cars, just what you can learn from books, so I don't know what kind it was. It was nearly six paces long and pointed at the corners. It had no roof, just a canvas canopy rigged over the open seats. The windshield was gone, and the upholstery was slashed down to a waxy yellow foam that must have once stuffed the cushions. Despite its disrepair, the wild boys had guarded their car well. It still had four wheels, flat tires and all, and the canopy seemed sturdy enough to keep the rain off.

We traded worried glances. Red watched us and smiled.

"Seen enough?" he asked. "We can come back later if you want to. But now it's time."

Lindy muttered, "Time for what, exactly?"

Red beamed at her. "Time for the party."

"Woo!" cried Zeke.

The other wild boys made a lot of similar noise. With flailing arms, cartwheels, and somersaults, they hauled us back into the room with the fire. The pigeons, now burned almost black, were still roasting. From some storage area downstairs more refreshments arrived, including a stoneware crock of clear liquid that smelled flammable.

"What's that stuff?" I asked as Red took a drink from the narrow neck of the jug.

"Potato brandy," Red replied. He wiped his mouth on the back of his hand and gave the jug's neck a rub with his fingers before he held it out to me. "Want some?"

"No, thanks," I said. From the look of the dirt on the jug, even if it didn't give me the pestilence, I thought it might give me something almost as bad.

The pigeons came off the spit. The wild boys offered us one, which Bud and King shared between them, and tore the rest into wings and legs. First they ate the meat, then they tossed the bones at each other. They seemed to enjoy the meal, shrieking with laughter and getting greasier with every bone they threw.

The only wild boys who didn't join in were Wilson and Red. Red stayed close to Toby. His eyes never met hers, but from time to time, as he watched the wild boys play, he leaned close to say a few words to her.

Wilson sat beside the fire with Esteban. Despite the uproar caused by the other wild boys' table manners, he seemed to notice nothing but Esteban's voice.

Esteban looked at Wilson. "You see the fire, don't you?"

Wilson nodded.

"Watch the fire burn, Wilson. When I count three, you'll look away from the fire. You'll be home. All will be well."

Wilson nodded again.

"One. Two. Three." Esteban's voice was gentle but firm.

Wilson looked from the fire to Esteban, his eyes filled with curiosity. "That was interesting," he said. "Like being awake and dreaming."

"Do you think so?" asked Esteban, pleased. "It takes me that way, too."

Wilson eyed Esteban with admiration. "Where did you learn to do that?" he asked. "Can you teach me?"

Esteban looked at the wild boys playing all around us, then back at Wilson. "It's sort of a knack," he replied. "You can probably teach yourself. Practice is the best of all instructors."

Spike came to sit between Lindy and me. "Nice warm spot to spend the night, anyway," he said, stretching his feet toward the fire. "Almost as good as the engine room."

"Almost as noisy," said Lindy. "Hey, Tomcat, that one does a cartwheel better than you do."

It took all my self-control not to look, but I kept my attention on Lindy. "I'm sure there are a lot of things this gang can do better than I can," I said. "Like eat glass and walk on nails."

"They can go quieter in the dark than you, that's for sure." Lindy smirked. "Spike, you should have heard us coming over with Esteban and Wilson. Tomcat would take three steps and then stub his toes — you never heard such hissing. He sounded like the valves on the *Rat*."

The wild boys, from somewhere, produced sticks, pipes, buckets, and cans. For a moment we all came on guard at the sight of possible weapons, but the wild boys only banged them together to make a lurching din. After a few moments, the noise settled into a steady rhythm and the wild boys began to dance. We exhaled slowly and relaxed again.

Spike had no trouble following the pattern of the noise. First he just tapped one foot in sympathy, but soon he was nodding in full approval. "Listen to that kid with the bucket and the hammer," he said. "Esteban, can I borrow your club?"

"No, you may not," said Esteban without looking up from his conversation with Wilson.

"Maybe they've got another hammer someplace," said Spike wistfully. He got up to go see.

"Exit Spike. That's the last we'll see of him for a while," Lindy said, and sighed. She held her hands out to the fire. "Hungry? There are a couple of pieces of pigeon left."

"No," I said. "Burnt pigeon might not do us any harm, but I don't like the idea of eating or drinking anything we didn't bring with us from the *Rat*."

"You think they want to poison us?" Lindy asked us. "If they do, the joke's on them. We've eaten your cooking so long, we're probably immune."

I leaned close, so that Lindy could catch my whisper without letting anyone else see my lips. "Pestilence," I hissed.

Lindy laughed. "Are you kidding? You're still worried about the pestilence? We're prisoners of the dreaded wild boys now, Tomcat. What makes you think we'll live long enough to get sick?"

I looked at the wild boys, dancing barefoot all around us. "They're not so terrible," I said.

Lindy smiled at me. She has a wonderful smile, full of joy and wickedness. "You're as bad as Spike," she said. "Do you want to dance, too? Or would you rather just sit here and watch and maybe drink some wild boy wine?"

I grimaced. "Now that stuff *is* poison, if you ask me."

"Oh, I doubt it," Lindy replied. "It doesn't seem to be doing King any harm."

I followed her gaze to where Bud and King were sitting side by side, passing a jug back and forth.

"Too bad it isn't poison, then. Bud's been drinking it, too," I said.

Lindy smirked. "Yeah, you can tell by the color in his face. He looks like a boiled beet. He'll be sorry in the morning."

"You think they brought us in here just to spend the night?" I asked.

Lindy shrugged. "I think they brought us here to give us a nice party," she said. "Afterward I think we aren't going to be good for much. Might as well see where we are in the morning and make plans then."

"What kind of thing is that to do — give us a nice party. Where's the sense in that?"

Lindy flipped her hand to indicate the dancing chaos in the center of the room. "Every night is Halloween on Puggy's Hill."

"What's that supposed to mean?" I demanded. "It's not Halloween yet."

Lindy sighed. "It's out of a storybook, Tomcat."

The noise of sticks and pipes had settled into a steady tattoo. With Spike's help on bucket and hammer, they were holding pretty close to six-eight time. On the other side of the fire, six or seven wild boys in a row were dancing a complicated step dance, arms across one another's shoulders, bare feet moving in a blur.

"That looks hard," I said.

Lindy followed my gaze. "Yeah, it does," she said after a long look. "What do you think? Could we do that? Shall we try it?"

"Try it?" I echoed. "We'll improve on it."

And so we did. And we did and we did, and that's how the rest of that night went.

WHEN I AWOKE the next morning, it took me a moment to remember where I was, and another to think of a good reason to move. I ached. The soles of my feet were sore from all the walking we'd done the day before. My toes and shins hurt from my encounters with railroad ties in the dark. Every other pain in my body, I put down to the dance the wild boys and Lindy and I had danced the night before. Except my left elbow. I couldn't imagine how I managed to bruise that. Finally, my stomach ached, since I had neither eaten nor drunk since the day before. It was the thought of my water flask that finally got me up. As quietly as possible I reached for my pack and opened it. To my delight there was a leathery piece of smoked trout in my rations that I'd forgotten all about. I took a pull at the water flask and sat down cross-legged to eat breakfast.

The chamber was still. The fire was nothing but a heap of gray ashes. The crazy tilt of papered wood leaning against the walls let in lines and wedges of sunlight to reveal huddled sleepers everywhere. Spike and Esteban were asleep on either side of Toby. Lindy was beside me, making the soft buzzing noise she won't admit is snoring. King had fallen asleep with his hand still on Red's jug of potato brandy. There were wild boys everywhere. But I didn't see Bud.

I popped the last little bit of smoked trout into my mouth and rose, chewing industriously. My first few steps were fairly creaky, but by the time I pushed through the canvas curtain and walked up to the roof, I was back to normal.

After days of rain and overcast, the autumn sky was clear blue from horizon to horizon. Overhead it was so dark a blue that I was surprised not to see stars. I yawned, stretched, and admired the view all around me.

From sixty feet up, the city looked even worse than it did from the ground, because I could see over some of the broken walls. Inside the ruined buildings were tangles of wreckage. It took me a moment to get my bearings so I could try to find the *Rat*. I leaned against the wall at the right spot and craned my neck, but there was a large piece of a shiny black building in the way. Though I couldn't spot the *Rat*, I could see the river, at least a snatch of it. There was a bend visible off to my left, well upstream of the *Rat*'s mooring place. The water reflected the sky's dark blue. It was going to be a nice day. Maybe even a warm one.

Except for the car, the roof was empty. I thought the spiral looked interesting. As I passed the car to follow it down, Bud's voice spoke from under the canopy: "Don't bother walking down. There's a sentry at the bottom. You'll only have to walk all the way back up, like I did."

I peered under the canopy into the back seat of the car. Bud was stretched out on the ripped foam, arms folded behind his head. Instead of the beet color he'd had the night before, his face was pale, almost bluish in the morning light. He was too tall to fit across the seat, so his boots were propped on the edge of the broken window. He crossed his ankles and slumped down even farther. He should have looked uncomfortable, or at least out of place. He didn't. He looked like he'd been born there.

"Thanks," I said. I tried the door to the front seat. It was jammed. I climbed over the door and settled down in the driver's seat. "I got plenty of exercise yesterday."

Bud grunted. "I know. I saw you. Dancing with those savages like you were one of them. Who are those kids, anyway? Who do they think they are, snatching us like that?"

"They're wild boys," I said. "They aren't so bad." There were three pedals on the floor on the driver's side of the car. I stepped on them one at a time. They didn't do anything.

"Yeah, I know they're wild boys," Bud replied. "But who are they? Where are they from? They can't live here. They'd freeze in this place come winter."

"They look pretty tough to me. Anyway" — I gestured to the city around us — "they've got the place to themselves. I expect they can find some way to keep warm."

"And there's not one of them over sixteen," Bud continued. "Where do they go when they get older?"

"They don't get older," I said. "They freeze out every winter, just like you said."

"Well, I don't like it."

"Oh. Well, that's different. If you don't like it, that changes everything."

"What are they *doing* here? That's what I want to know," Bud went on, ignoring me. "They're healthy, they're strong — when I was their age, I'd been milking every morning and night for five years."

"No cows here. And if the folks in Pig's Eye know anything about it, that's exactly why the wild boys are here. No cows."

Bud gave up his lazy pose and leaned over my seat, glaring at me. "What do cows have to do with anything?"

"You're the one who dragged cows into it," I replied. "All I mean is that these kids are here because they don't want to take orders. They don't want to spend their lives milking cows night and morning. They'd rather take their chances here than live in a place like Pig's Eye or Bass City or Rose Hill."

That shut Bud up for a while. I fiddled with the ring dangling from the key in the car's ignition until he spoke again. "Well, okay," he said grudgingly, "but why is it only wild boys and no wild girls?"

"Girls don't run away to be alone," I replied.

"The hell they don't," Bud retorted. "If you knew any girls, you'd know better than that."

"All right," I conceded, "girls run away, but they know how to work together. So if they're in a group, they work as a group. The wild boys just spend time together, they don't really *do* anything. Imagine if they cooperated. They'd be dangerous."

There was another long pause. Then, in a low nervous voice, Bud asked, "That Lindy, what about him?"

I sat up straight. "What about Lindy?" I demanded.

"Well . . ." Bud hesitated, then said, "he's not a him, is he? He's a her. Isn't she? Listen, do you two get it on, or what?"

One Lester I could handle, I thought. If he had ideas, I might be able to cure him of them before he annoyed Lindy. But then what? I considered how this whole conversation would probably sound to Lindy and winced. "What gave you the idea Lindy's a girl?" I asked.

"She's got kind of skinny shoulders," Bud replied. "For a guy to be that good at fighting, you'd expect better shoulders. Haven't you noticed?"

I didn't know what to say to that, so I kept my eyes on the key ring and finally said, "I think you better discuss this with Lindy."

"Well, I don't understand you guys at all," Bud replied. "If she was my girl, I wouldn't tell you to discuss it with her. I wouldn't just sit there."

I spread my hands and put them carefully on the steering wheel, where they couldn't do anything without my permission. "Listen, I don't know what you're used to," I said gently, "though from what I hear, I have to say I think Rose Hill stinks. But I'm from the *River Rat*, not Noah's Ark. There's no law I ever heard of that says people have to travel in pairs. Lindy does what

Lindy wants to do, I do what I want to do, you do what you want to do—"

"I get the idea," said Bud. "Well," he said, sounding surprised and satisfied at the same time, "that's good news. Do you think she likes me?"

I looked at Bud. His color was back and he looked more like Lester than I'd ever noticed before. He licked his lips. Thick lips.

"You should ask Lindy that," I said. I stood up and vaulted out of the car. "I'll go wake her up for you." Because she's going to cream you and I want to watch, I thought.

Bud got up quickly. "Don't do that. I don't want her to know I'm interested yet."

I ignored Bud and went in to find Lindy. She and Spike were still sleeping soundly. A few wild boys were up and stirring. Someone had hung a bucket of soup over the rekindled fire. Toby was studying a ladleful of it.

"Smells good," I said.

Toby sniffed at the grayish liquid and poured it back into the bucket. "Somebody picked up all those bones they were throwing around last night."

"I guess it doesn't smell so good after all."

"I guess not," said Toby. "Have you been looking around?"

"I was up on the roof. Bud says there's a sentinel posted at the foot of the spiral ramp."

"Have you looked around downstairs?"

"Not yet."

Toby stirred the bucket of soup again, without seeming to see it. "Take a look now," she said. "Who knows what Bud thinks he's doing here?"

"Who knows indeed," I said and went to look around downstairs.

I found my way to the door where we'd come in the night before. The metal panel was open. There was the clearance sign and the crossbar. Zeke was back in his chair in the booth, but all he did was wave until I went near the open door.

"Going someplace?" he called.

I turned and looked at him curiously. "Would you let me go?"

"Red said to leave you alone," Zeke said. He let his chair down on all four legs and sauntered over to me. "Where you going?"

"I'm just looking around," I replied.

"Well, it's kind of boring out there," Zeke said. "If you want me to, I'll let you go, but it's better here."

"We could just go?"

"You? Sure. Not your friends, though. Been downstairs yet?"

"I thought this was downstairs," I said. "Why not my friends?"

Zeke smiled. "I don't know. Red says so. Come this way. I'll show you something."

I followed Zeke past the booth and into the shadows at the foot of the ramp. There, half hidden by a stack of scrap lumber, was a door with a slogan sprayed in black over peeling yellow enamel: Awtherized Wild Boyz Only Beyund This Point. Zeke opened the door. From the darkness beyond came a smell of damp stone and cool earth.

"What's down there?" I asked.

"Caves," said Zeke. "You don't think we live up here all winter, do you?" He looked down, then back at me.

"No, I guess not," I said. "Why is it so dark down there?"

Zeke found that question very funny. "Because there isn't any light." I tried to laugh with him but gave up long before he did.

"Well, I'm not an Authorized Wild Boy," I said finally. "Maybe I shouldn't go down there."

"You could be if you wanted. Red says so."

"Oh, well, if Red says so, I guess it's okay." Wondering what I'd done to make Red single me out, I took a step into the dark. I didn't want to go down there. But I *really* didn't want Zeke to know I didn't want to. And I was still busy figuring what the offer to join the wild boys meant. So I took one step and stopped.

"If you'd rather wait till we light the lamps tonight, I understand. I don't like the dark, either," said Zeke.

"I'm not scared of the dark," I said, stung. And I'm not. I don't know what it was about those steps that bothered me. Maybe the damp smell.

"Oh, me neither," said Zeke. "I just don't like it, that's all."

"Then I won't make you go down there with me." I came back and helped Zeke conceal the door with scrap lumber again.

"I'll take you down tonight when we've got lamps," Zeke promised.

"Great," I said. "I'll go tell my friends."

"Well, if you want to," said Zeke. "But Red only talked about *you*. You should think about joining us. You dance like a wild boy already."

WHEN I GOT back, Toby was still stirring the soup. Lindy and Spike were gone. Esteban was trying to explain the discipline of breath to Wilson.

"Where's Lindy? Where's Spike?" I asked, dropping down beside Toby.

"I sent them up to the roof. They're working on something for me."

"I thought wild boys were supposed to be dangerous," I said. "They're a lot friendlier than I expected. They won't let us go, but they want me to join up."

"Red tells me they watched us come in on the *River Rat*. I think he wants a ride."

"Great," I said, disgusted. "More passengers."

"More bad luck," said Toby. She let the ladle go. "Come on. Help me wake up the old guy."

King, prone on his crumpled blanket, his face buried in his folded arms, snored richly.

"King," said Toby, shaking his arm, "it's time to get up." She shook him again, harder. "It's time to eat."

King uttered a strangled moan. "Go away. I'm sick."

Toby picked up a metal cup beside King's blanket and sniffed at the contents. "Whose fault is that?" she asked as she emptied the cup into the fire.

With a muffled *whump* and a blue flash, the liquid burned in an instant.

"What was that?" I demanded.

"Potato brandy," Toby replied.

If it burned like that, I wondered how it tasted. "*That's* the stuff you and Bud were drinking last night?"

King rolled over and glared at us. "Why don't you kids just leave me alone? Now I'll be awake all day."

"That's the idea," said Toby. She got to her feet. "We're leaving."

"They won't let us leave," King said. "They're going to keep us here. Probably they plan to fatten us up and eat us."

"Don't give them any ideas," said Toby.

We each took an elbow. Together, Toby and I got King on his feet. The wild boys paid no attention as we led him to the roof.

There the hood of the car was up and most of Spike was inside with the engine. To lift the hood, Lindy and Bud had untied the tangle of ropes and cables, which they were busy coiling. Lindy looked cross. Bud's face was scarlet and there was a lump on his jaw I didn't remember seeing before. I realized I'd missed his conversation with Lindy.

Toby left me with King while she ventured under the hood to consult with Spike. Then she emerged, went back below, and returned with the jug of potato brandy, Zeke and Red at her heels.

Zeke put his head under the hood, next to Spike's. "Think you can fix the engine?"

Spike's hair was on end, his hands black with grease. "Fix it? I'm not even sure I can find it. Where's that hammer you had last night?" Spike wiped his hands on the seat of his pants and went deeper under the hood.

Zeke left to look for the hammer. Wistfully I watched him go. No meetings for the wild boys, I thought. No common law and constitutional government. Just give an order and they take it. It would save a lot of time, being a wild boy. Of course, before they let you give them an order, you have to get their attention.

Red turned to Toby. "Great car, isn't it?"

Toby nodded. "It's a classic."

"Of course," Red added, "it needs a lot of work."

Toby nodded without taking her eyes off Spike's legs.

Muffled, Spike's voice came from beneath the hood. "There's juice left in this battery, I think. The points are a disgrace, though. Hand me that stuff."

His grimy hand emerged, and Toby handed him the jug of potato brandy.

"Our friend here isn't feeling well," Toby told Red, pointing to King. Her chatty voice was back. The slow, gentle tone she used made me listen hard. There was more to her words than their first meaning. Something was up.

King looked a little pale, not as bad as Bud, but definitely a little green. "I think he needs somewhere to sit down," Toby said to Red. "Will you help Tomcat get him into the back seat?"

Red took King's free elbow and the two of us wedged him into the back seat.

"Esteban," said Toby, "put the front seat forward more so King has enough room in back, will you? He's not feeling well, you know."

Esteban climbed awkwardly into the front seat and released the catch on the seat while Red and I pushed forward. When the seat had gone as far as it could, Esteban crooked his good arm over the back of the seat and turned to inspect King. After a long critical look, he shook his head sadly. "The impulse of wrong desire is the greatest enemy to the happiness of man."

"Ain't that the truth," I said, eyeing Bud.

King ignored us both. So did Bud. Lindy gave me an inscrutable look and went back to coiling cable.

"Finished," called Spike, handing the jug back to Toby.

Toby took it. As she moved to set it down, I thought she handled it easier than when she'd brought it to Spike. She put both hands on the driver's door and hopped into the seat. "Spike?"

"Do it," Spike called back.

Toby turned the key in the ignition. After a moment, there was a noise like a groan from beneath the hood. Spike's feet jerked as he plunged even farther into the motor, fighting for a response from the machine.

The engine caught with a roar and Spike shot out from under the hood.

"Get in!" shouted Toby. She stomped on the pedals like she was trying to kill a snake. The roar of the engine gentled for a moment and the car jerked forward.

Bud and Lindy dropped their coils of rope and leapt to the trunk of the car as Red and I sprang into the back seat. King made a strangled noise of protest as we landed on him. The car lurched ahead on its ruined tires.

"I did it, I did it!" Spike did a quick excited little dance alongside the car, then vaulted into the front seat on top of Toby. "Let it out slow!"

The engine roared fiercely again.

"Slow!" Spike yelled.

The engine howled, then gave a cough and died. We were still moving slowly, but it was just the last of our momentum carrying us forward. For an awful moment we sat, a silent tangle of bodies heaped into the car. The brief life Spike breathed into the motor had lasted only long enough for us to pull out from under the canopy.

Spike gave a cry of frustration and dropped his head in his hands. Beneath him Toby struggled to get free.

Red stirred next to me. "That wasn't so good after all," he said.

Although the engine was dead, the car was still rolling very slowly. We reached the steep spiral ramp. Gravity did what potato brandy couldn't. We began to coast downward.

Toby was still struggling with Spike. "Move your head. I can't see anything."

"Hold *still*, Toby. I can't reach the pedals when you do that!" Spike yelled. He hauled on the steering wheel with all his weight, trying to keep the car from scraping the outer wall of the ramp. "Keep her in neutral."

"Which pedal is neutral?" Toby shrieked back.

From her spot on the trunk of the car Lindy pounded my shoulder. "Ever hear Toby scream before?" she demanded gleefully.

I started to say no and got a mouthful of Red's white hair. I spat it out and clean forgot what I was going to say. Despite the wrecked tires, the car was gaining momentum as we descended.

Spike's grip on the steering wheel couldn't keep the car in the center of the ramp. With a spray of sparks the right fender scraped the wall. Toby added her strength to Spike's. The scraping stopped and we headed toward the left wall.

Red elbowed me in the ribs as he scrambled to his knees for a better view of our descent. He looked pleased and excited. We scraped the left wall. I closed my eyes. It didn't help. Though I couldn't see the sparks, I could still hear the scrape of metal on concrete. I opened my eyes. We bounced toward the right wall and scraped again. We seemed to be gaining speed.

Lindy was still pounding my shoulder. Bud was swearing, the same few words over and over. King was moaning, but I don't think he was afraid; I think he was being smothered under Red and me. With his good hand Esteban was trying to help with the steering wheel.

Near the bottom of the ramp the slope flattened out. We were going much too fast for that to make any difference. Ahead I could see that the metal panel was still open. There was the clearance sign. And the crossbar was still down.

"Everybody duck!" Spike shouted.

Red elbowed me again. Bud tried to crawl in the back seat on top of us. Lindy flattened herself across as much of the trunk as she could reach. Esteban and Toby and Spike did their best to crouch.

As we sailed toward him, I saw Zeke on duty in the booth. His chair was tilted comfortably back.

The car was bigger than I thought. It clipped the crossbar as we came, and the red metal crumpled like paper. Zeke smiled and waved at us as we shot past. He didn't even let his chair down on all four legs. Beside me Red waved back at him.

The car left the ramp behind and headed full speed for the street.

In one long instant I saw the sky and the sun, Red's hair, and Lindy's hand clinging to the back seat next to Bud's.

There was a bone-jarring crash. The car hit some rubble and stopped.

We kept going a moment longer, just the fraction of a second it took to land in a knot of arms and legs. The impact was chaos, but through it all I could hear Red shouting, "It works!" and Spike shouting, "I did it!"

My face was mashed into the slashed upholstery and some-one was sitting on my legs. Otherwise I felt fine. The car wasn't moving — that was the main thing.

Toby pushed Spike out of the front seat and into the street, then turned to pull Esteban up and out of the car. Lindy and Bud had been thrown into the back seat on top of Red and King and me. Red, I was fairly sure, was the weight on my legs. The heap of us was slow to untangle.

"Where's King?" Toby demanded.

"His foot is in my stomach," Bud replied.

Someone bent my arm the wrong way and wriggled free. It was Bud. He reached back to help Lindy. Lindy ignored him and found King's other foot. With help from me, they got the old guy upright and out of the car. By the time I was able to see over the back seat, Toby had our group gathered together and was herd-ing them all into a run. Red was climbing on the trunk of the car, calling his wild boys, who were running down the ramp after us with coils of rope and cable. They were shouting and punching each other. They looked excited. I hauled myself out, staggered, and went after Toby and the others.

Behind me Red's voice lifted. "It's a classic! Get it back up there and we'll do it again."

I snatched a glance back as I ran. The wild boys were at the car, uncoiling ropes and cables. Red supervised as they swarmed around him. They looked like they were getting ready to push the car back up the spiral. Busy with this new project, no one paid any attention to our departure.

I tripped on a brick, stumbled, and caught my balance. With no pursuit to worry me, I set my mind on catching up with my companions.

9

A WALK IN
THE COUNTRY

E RAN THROUGH THE CITY; WE jogged through the pillars beneath the overpass; we limped westward into empty streets and the wreckage of old fires. We ran until King let out a long groan. He stopped and bent nearly double in the middle of the crumbled road. He looked to me like he was deciding which of his shoes to lace first. When he got enough breath back to talk, he said, "Oh, the hell with it," and sat down in the road.

I stopped. The road behind us was empty. Ahead, the others had noticed King's surrender. One by one, they slowed until they had gathered in a knot, gesturing and urging us to join them. I sat down next to King and listened to him wheeze while the others debated what to do. Finally they came back to join us. The seven of us sat in a ring on the cracked asphalt.

"That car was great," said Spike. "I bet I could get it to run pretty good if I could just charge that battery." He put his elbows on his knees and his chin in his hands. "Wonder if a Never Ready would do the trick."

Bud looked disgusted, but he didn't say anything. His bluish look had come back.

"How much farther?" Lindy asked King.

King shrugged.

"How far are we from the *River Rat* now?" I asked. "All this running around confuses me."

"Perhaps three miles," Esteban said. He got to his feet. "We make haste slowly. Each step we take away from the *Rat* brings us the sooner home."

Toby rose. "Then let's take steps."

We hadn't traveled far before Lindy began to sing as she marched: *"Oh, I wish I was first-mate on board a man-o'-war, say I'm going away on board a man-o'-war. Pretty work, brave boys, pretty work I say, I'm going away on board a man-o'-war."*

We took turns making up the first line. Toby always wished to be something to do with ships, like captain. Lindy always chose something that scanned. Spike always chose something mechanical, like engineer. Esteban always chose something he really wished for — *Oh, I wish I was enlightened on board a man-o'-war* — whether it made sense or not.

Everyone sang the chorus except Bud.

King got into the spirit of things right away, although he sang as slowly as he walked. Bud didn't sing at all. When it was my turn, I sang that I wished I was a wild boy on board a man-o'-war. Esteban shook his head and looked disappointed.

WE WALKED UNTIL the sun was low before us and our shadows came after like black ribbons. The road was not memorable. It rose and fell, but not much. When it rose, the soft soil on either side grew wiry grass and Queen Anne's lace and goldenrod. When it fell, reeds rustled so close to the road it was like walking through a swamp.

We stopped for the night on one of the rises, a spot that had only the view going for it. As far as we could see in either direction, the road was clear. The wiry grass grew high enough to conceal a careful pursuer, so we knew we weren't truly safe; but it was the best spot the ground offered. We took sentry duty in turn. There was nothing in the quiet night to trouble us. It was clear, with a waning moon rising late. The stars spangled the dark overhead. Lindy and I took turns inventing new constellations for ourselves: the Rudder, the Sounding Pole, and the Soup Ladle.

The moon was still shining in the west when the sun rose and we got ready to go on. Careful of our limited supplies, we made a poor breakfast of oatcakes and a swallow of water. When King was sure it was light enough that he could not miss his way, we set forth.

King looked better than he had the day before, as if the long walk had worked the potato brandy out of his system. Bud looked worse than ever. Still pale, he was greasy with sweat, and despite our light meals, he often had to stop to relieve himself.

I caught Esteban taking careful looks at Bud as we walked along. Once I caught King staring at Bud. Then King and Esteban stared at each other for a moment, but neither said anything. I considered asking a stupid question to get them to talk about whatever was wrong. But I decided that the answer to the stupid question would only be "Shut up, Tomcat." So I kept quiet.

In the middle of the afternoon Esteban halted, his head up in a way that made us all stop and look at him with interest.

"Somebody's coming," he said.

It was stupid just to stand there and wait, but the grass gave us no cover. We waited in silence. Another moment and we could all hear what Esteban had caught at a distance, a ringing sound like steel scraping stone. Over the next small rise in the road came a brown horse with a rider. As we watched, the rider came within ten yards of us and stopped.

"You there," called the rider, in a voice that tried to sound stern but couldn't help sounding happy and satisfied instead. "Stand and deliver."

We stood and stared.

"Deliver what?" Spike muttered behind me.

"It's out of a book," Lindy muttered back. "It means stick 'em up."

The rider was a woman, older than Bud, wearing khaki trousers and shirt. Her face was broad and ruddy, eyes bright with amusement. She had light brown hair, the same color as Bud's, but hers fell long and loose past her shoulders. The breeze lifted it as she sat watching us from the saddle and brushed it across her face. When she put up her hand to push her hair back, I saw she wore long gloves of worn red leather. On horseback she looked as big and strong as a Lester. We stared at her and she studied us, half laughing, until the horse shook its head. The bit and bridle jingled. The rider laughed aloud.

"I always wanted to say that. Stand and deliver," she repeated.

"She's old and she's big, but she doesn't look too tough to

me," said Lindy softly. "Tomcat, if we have to fight, do what you can to spook the horse."

"How?"

"Oh, I don't know. Sing something."

Of all of us, Bud and King were staring the hardest.

Bud rubbed his forehead as if it ached. King rubbed the back of his neck.

"Becky?" Bud asked hoarsely, "Is that you?"

King didn't wait for her to answer. "What in the wild blue world are you doing here?" he snarled. "Don't you know by now that I'm not safe to be around? How did you get here—and where did that thing come from?" He looked at the horse with dislike.

Becky moved the horse forward. Closer to us, she didn't have to raise her voice to answer King. "I stole it. That's a hanging offense back in Rose Hill, but it was the only way I could think of to get here before Lester and the boys brought you. I figured I could maybe be there to help you out a little. Or maybe just stay and learn how to run the generator." She looked from King to the rest of us. Even when she wasn't laughing, I could see the crinkles set at the outer corners of her eyes. "I know Bud," she said slowly. "Who are all the rest of you?"

"Officious brats who won't do as they're told," King replied. "Same as you."

"You're in trouble and it's my fault. What did you expect me to do?" Becky shook her head. "You didn't really expect me to listen to that 'far, far better' stuff, did you?"

"I didn't expect you to leap out of the shrubbery at me either," said King. He looked peeved.

Becky looked sheepish. "I got bored," she said. "It's hard to hide a horse. They get lonesome and then they make noise. And they eat all the time. I figured it was safe to come out of hiding when I saw Lester wasn't with you."

"Pa will kill you when he catches you," said Bud. He was still rubbing his forehead. He sounded hoarse, like he'd been coughing for about an hour.

"Lester won't catch me," Becky said.

Bud took his hand away from his forehead and stumbled forward, reaching to Becky.

"Don't get too close," warned Becky. "This horse bites."

Bud fell headlong on the road. The horse shied and danced away from him. Bud lay still. We all moved forward. King got to Bud first. With Spike's help, he rolled him over. Bud was so pale he was gray, and his breath scraped in his throat, an ugly sound.

Becky, red gloves hard on the reins, steadied the horse. I watched her watch King as he examined Bud. Her forehead was puckered, all trace of laughter gone from her face. She and the horse were so still they could have been a statue.

King looked up at Esteban, then across Bud at Toby. His voice was as gentle as his hands on Bud's face and shoulder. "This kid is *real* sick. It could be neotyphus — what you kids call the pestilence."

Toby looked down at Bud. "What do you think we should do?"

"Leave him," said Spike. He looked at Bud fearfully. "We could leave him."

"We could," said Esteban, "but what if you're the next one to catch it, Spike? Should we leave you?"

"If I catch it, you ought to leave me," Spike said. "The pestilence will hold us up, and Lester didn't give us all winter to get back to Jake, you know."

"Spike has a point," said Lindy.

King looked very tired. "Don't waste your breath debating, kids. You can't go anywhere without me and I won't leave Bud like this."

"You've got a point there," Spike admitted.

"Thank God for that. We can skip the voice vote," King said. He looked at Becky astride her horse. "Will you let us borrow that animal?"

Becky's eyes were on Bud. "Is he going to die?" She sounded stern.

King said, "I don't know. Could be. Will you help us?"

"Will I catch it?" Becky asked.

King snarled, "I don't know. I don't know everything."

Becky studied him and her mouth relaxed a little. "I know that," she said. The horse sidled. She urged it closer to Bud. "Put him in front of me," she said. "I'll hold him, and the horse will keep up with you."

We wrapped Bud in his blanket and got him across the horse. The horse didn't like the idea. I had to hold the bridle while the others pushed and pulled Bud into place. Just as they got him balanced, the horse moved its head and bit my stomach. I let go of the bridle and leapt backward, more surprised than hurt.

"I warned you," said Becky. She had the reins in hand again. The horse walked forward stiffly, as if all four legs had just turned to wood. Becky made it head back the way she'd come. "If we're going to the Pharaoh's tomb," she said harshly, "let's get on with it and go."

King set off. She followed. The rest of us did too. As I walked, I lifted my shirt to inspect the damage the horse had done. There was a red welt a few inches above my navel, but the skin wasn't broken. I rubbed the welt and said, "I always thought they ate grass."

AT SUNDOWN KING put his hand on the horse's neck. Becky stopped the horse and bent toward King.

"No farther," King said. He put his hand on Bud's face for a moment. When he took it away, he looked grim. "We can't go on until morning. If we pass the place in the dark, I'll never find it."

"I think he's worse," Becky said.

"You're right," said King. "He is. I'm sorry. We'll have to do the best we can here. I know how you feel about him."

Becky looked surprised. "I doubt it. I'm not sure I know myself. He's my cousin. But he punched me in the stomach every day for about three years, until I got brave enough to punch him back."

It was King's turn to look surprised. "I thought you were his sister."

"I have a lot of brothers, and even more cousins," Becky replied. "Plenty of uncles, too."

King's eyes narrowed. "What did he say when you punched him?"

"He didn't say anything. He just found somebody smaller to punch instead."

"But you and the smaller kid stuck together, right?" Spike demanded.

Becky's frown turned to a scowl. "That's not how it works back home. Lester doesn't like people who take sides. So people don't. Hold this horse while we get Bud down, will you?"

King made me hold the horse. I kept a tighter grip on the bridle this time. The horse didn't try to bite me, but I got my hands all slimy from the bit. Horses are disgusting.

We made camp right there beside the road. Spike and I ranged far enough to find some firewood in a stand of scrubby trees, but we were limited to what we could find as deadfall, since we had no hatchet, only a knife Becky had loaned us. The armfuls of firewood didn't last long. While Esteban and King took turns trying to doctor Bud, the rest of us helped with the camp. We were either standing guard, sleeping, or scouring what brush there was for more firewood. It was not a good night.

BY MORNING, BUD was too sick to move. We spent the day the same way we spent the night, gathering firewood against the cold and dark to come. Nobody said much. Partly we were tired. Partly we were worried.

If anything happened to Bud, what would happen to Jake? What if Bud gave it to us? If he did, I thought I'd kill him . . . if the pestilence didn't get him first.

And partly, at least for me, there was the squirm of guilt. I didn't like Bud. Whatever happened to him, it wasn't going to make me feel as bad as it ought to.

There was nothing to say. There was a lot to do. So I shut up and concentrated on keeping the fire going.

Bud's fever went higher and higher as the night wore on. He vomited blood about midnight. The moon rose late. By that time Bud was still. Only his fever was strong. By the time the moon was overhead, Bud's pulse was too faint to feel. We couldn't tell exactly when he died, but he was cold to the touch by morning.

We had to bury him at the edge of the marsh. That was the only spot soft enough to let us dig a grave with just our hands and Becky's long knife. Becky cut rushes to line the shallow ditch.

While she worked, Toby and Lindy wrapped the body in Bud's blanket.

"That's a perfectly good blanket," Spike said.

"Oh, yeah? Do you want to use it? I don't," Lindy replied.

"Better not," King said. "With neotyphus, you never know. You kids are probably less susceptible than Becky and Bud because you've had more exposure to strangers. Me too. Rose Hill is a closed environment. But you never know. Better take no chances."

Toby looked up. "Lend a hand, Tomcat. Easy now."

We laid the body in the grave. It took a while. I was glad of the rushes. It would have seemed wrong just to put the body down in the dirt.

Esteban waited until we were standing beside him at the edge of the grave. Then he bowed his head and we did the same. I thought at first that he was going to say a prayer or something, but he didn't. We just stood, heads bowed in silence, for a minute or more.

Toby touched Becky's arm. The rest of us set to work filling in the grave. When it was covered with earth, Becky scattered more rushes over the top. When she was done, she sat down next to the grave and put her face in her hands. She sat that way for a long time. Her shoulders shook a little, but she made no sound and her breathing was almost steady. The rest of us stood awkwardly, trying not to look impatient.

WE SET OFF again in the middle of the morning, grim and silent. Becky rode her horse in the lead. Toby and King walked on either side. At a careful distance — for we found it was no safer to walk behind the horse than it was to walk just in front of it — Lindy, Spike, Esteban, and I brought up the rear. We were footsore and too tired even to squabble, but I think we were all glad to be moving again. Anything was better than another hour there by the grave. We were worn out; but from what I could see, we showed only the signs of honest fatigue, not the bluish weariness Bud had displayed.

After a few miles, King suggested he and Becky ride ahead on the horse to find out how much farther it was to the tomb.

Toby's face twisted, but when she spoke her voice was level. "We stay together."

King took a look at Toby's expression and nodded. I think his agreement had something to do with the coldness in her eyes. I could guess what made her look that way. If King and Becky betrayed us, where were we? And even if they didn't, once Lester learned about Bud, what would happen to Jake?

We went on as we were, in total silence, for hours. The road curved southward. The reeds along the road to our left gradually became true marsh. King slowed, then stopped.

"Everything looks different," he said wearily. "That used to be a lake. I think."

"How much farther?" Spike asked.

King shrugged. "We have to come to a rise on our right. Then a road should run off to the north along the rise. At the end of the road there's a house. Beneath the house is the Pharaoh's tomb."

Lindy stuck her thumbs in her belt. "We've passed seven hundred rises already," she said. "Three hundred and fifty of them were on our left and all the rest were on our right."

I shook my water flask. From the sound I judged there might be as much as two whole swallows left. I put it back in my pack and thought wistfully of apples.

We set off again. In less than a mile, at the top of the next rise, King stopped abruptly. Before us on the left marsh turned into open water. On our right the rise ran north like a spine. King studied the ground at the edge of the crumbled road. As we watched him anxiously, he looked north, then back down at the road. Then, still silent, he set off along the spine of the little ridge, north into the wiry grass.

We followed. As we hurried after him, the horse put its head down to snatch bites of the long grass. Becky let it. She was intent on following King.

The ridge ran north until it reached a hollow, invisible from the road. There, weathered wreckage nearly filled a straight-sided hole in the ground — the foundation of a house. King paused at the edge of the hole, looked around swiftly, then let himself down amid the wreckage. He glanced back up at us as we ranged around the hole to watch. "We're here," he said. His voice was ragged. "This is the Pharaoh's tomb."

Standing a little crooked to ease his arm in its sling, his shoulders slumped with fatigue, Esteban watched King closely.

As he looked down, the afternoon sun caught the fire in his ear-ring. The ruby gleamed as he nodded to himself. He looked the way he had when the Lesters stormed the *River Rat*, as though he watched a horizon only he could see, a view that puzzled him and made him sad. "The longest way round is the shortest way home," he said.

We looked at Esteban, then back at King, who was frown-ing up at him. "More news from the lion of self-control?" King asked.

"We've helped you to your home," Esteban said. "Now we need your help to win back our own. But let us have some hon-esty first. Why have you never returned here? And why did you leave in the first place?"

King studied Esteban, then shrugged. "Ever hear of Pan-dora's box?"

"Of course," said Esteban. "It contained hope."

"Along with a thousand curses," King retorted. "Some say hope is the greatest curse of all."

"Hope is danger's comforter," said Esteban.

Spike and I looked at each other. He rolled his eyes and muttered, "I hate it when he talks like that."

Lindy whispered. "What's going on with these two, anyway?"

Toby cleared her throat. "Esteban wants King to admit he's the Pharaoh."

Esteban and King both scowled at Toby.

Toby said, "We don't have much time. We've got to get inside."

King turned his scowl on Esteban. "What gives you the idea *I'm* the Pharaoh?"

"Oh, several small things," Esteban replied. "'Loitering

with Intent, for one. Your name, King, for another. What I don't understand is, why did you leave?"

"I didn't," King replied. He looked around at the ruined foundation. "I wasn't here. I was on tour when the Flash came. It's taken me a long time to find my way back here."

"Why?" asked Esteban.

"I'm afraid to open the box," King answered. He looked up at Becky and stopped scowling. "I figured the only use I had for it was to crawl inside and not come out again. But after the Flash, I didn't want to bury myself, not even in my very own tailor-made tomb."

"Are you kidding?" Becky demanded. "If you have just half the stuff you told me about in there, you can run this place. You can be a *real* king."

King winced. "Not for long. You've seen just how tough I am. I don't have the spine to be a king. If the Lesters get the idea they want this stuff, they'll take it away from me. I don't have what it takes to argue with them."

Becky looked confused. "Lesters?"

"Later," said Toby.

King didn't pay any attention. "When the Flash came," he said, looking back into some memory that slowed his words, "I was on a tour bus west of Omaha. By the time we reached Omaha, the pestilence was there. Nobody knew where it came from — might have been the other side. But it could just as easily have been ours, something that got loose by mistake. Nobody knew for certain. Nobody knew anything for certain. Anyway, there was no way home through that. By the time I got out of Omaha, I knew I couldn't just open up the tomb and share supplies. People aren't like that."

"What did you know about people?" demanded Lindy. "My uncle Andy was a roadie for Memento Mori. From the stories he tells, a singer back then might as well have been living on the moon for all they had to do with normal people."

King smiled. "I considered living there," he said, "but the rent was way too high. As for people—I was in Omaha for the department store riots."

"Oh." Lindy looked impressed.

"So I couldn't go home and open the tomb to all comers," King continued, "and I couldn't come back and stay here all alone, either."

"Why not?" Spike demanded. "That's what I'd do."

"Would you? I wonder." King looked at Spike. "Would you lock yourself up alone after you made the trip across Nebraska, living on the food of people who had little enough to eat themselves, yet shared it with you? People who still believed that life had something to do with dignity? People," he added, "who seemed to think I could help them?"

"Well," said Spike slowly, "that's different."

"I thought so, too," said King. "I couldn't help them, not really. But my . . . my friend could. She was a doctor, a good one. Even at the worst, even when all she had to work with was a needle and thread, she could still heal people. Maybe it was her voice, I don't know. She *sounded* like she could help. I learned a little bit just by being with her." He was looking back into his memory again. "We got as far as Saint Louis. She went down with neotyphus herself and died about twelve hours later. No time for graves then, not even mass graves. They just burned the bodies where they lay. Sometimes—often—the fire got away and took the house, several houses . . ." He paused, swallowed,

163

and added, "Sometimes I wake up thinking I smell smoke. That same smoke. After all this time." He shrugged. "So after that, I know the pestilence when I see it, and I can set broken bones, and I can stitch up a cut if it isn't too bad."

"You lived through the days after the Flash," said Lindy, puzzled, "and yet you told Lester about the guns. How could you do that?"

King's mouth twisted. "Ask the lion of self-control there to tell you about the king's talking horse."

Esteban looked completely blank. "What?"

King smiled with great satisfaction. "Never read Herodotus? There's a story he tells about a slave who's been sentenced to death by a king. The slave says, 'Spare me and I'll teach your horse to talk. If I haven't succeeded in one year from today, you may put me to death.' The king decided he'd like his horse to talk, so he agreed to give the slave one year to perform the task. The other slaves said, 'Are you crazy?' But the bold slave said, 'Not at all. A lot can happen in a year. I might die. The king might die. Or, who knows? The horse might learn to talk.' Telling Lester about the guns was a gamble. But I hoped something might happen to stop them from catching me and finding out anything about the tomb's location. Or they might contract neotyphus on their way through town. Or, who knows? Lester might see the light and want the tomb for the useful things that are there, like the generator." His smile turned bitter again. "I might have known it was a vain hope. Most hope is."

"Sure," said Spike, "but what else have we got? Show us the way into this tomb of yours."

"We need to get to the center of this mess," said King. He spoke with sudden energy, as if he was glad to be finished with talk about the past. "Ought to be easy to find. There's a cube of reinforced concrete, about nine feet on a side. That houses the elevator. The default setting keeps the car at the bottom of the shaft, but there's a control panel with a digital code. I should be able to call it up as soon as we clear the doors. If I can remember the code."

"It's in code? Great. What kind?" demanded Spike.

"Just a nine-digit access code," King replied. "I used my social security number. But it's been a while since anybody asked me what my social security number is. I'm pretty sure I'll get it in a couple of tries, though."

Becky looked up from tethering the horse. "Social security?" she echoed uncertainly.

Toby met her puzzled look and shrugged. "Maybe Esteban knows what it is."

"If he does," replied King, "get him to explain it to me. If he can, the kid's a genius."

IT TOOK US until dusk to clear the doors of debris. When we finished, the control panel gave us no response, not even after half an hour's stabbing and swearing from King.

"I'm sure that's the number," he said, poking the neat plastic squares for the ninety-ninth time. "Got to be."

"Let Spike try," said Toby.

King looked huffy. "Why not? It's broken anyway."

By the light of a makeshift torch, Spike spent another half hour prying the control panel away and studying the panel behind it. Finally he looked up. "Semiconductors," he said, as if it was a bad word. "Sorry. Nothing to bang with a hammer."

"What's the matter with it?" Becky asked.

165

Spike shrugged. "It doesn't work."

"Oh." Becky looked from Spike to King, who was staring into the distance and muttering numbers to himself. "Those metal panels are the doors, huh?"

Scowling, King folded his arms. "Yes."

Becky picked up a lever-shaped piece of debris and fitted it into the edge of the door. "Well, let's open the doors, then."

"If it doesn't work, force it," Esteban said. "If it breaks, it needed fixing anyway."

King gave Esteban a long look, then nodded. "You're finally talking my language, kid. This elevator cost me a year's royalties. Ought to be in pieces before you can say Jackie Robinson."

"Who's Jackie Robinson?" asked Becky.

"Just use the lever," King said. He looked cross.

I don't know how much a year's royalty is, but if weight means anything, that elevator must have cost a lot. We were barely able to shift the doors enough to use Becky's lever. It took our entire combined strength to slide the metal panels back and expose the entrance to the Pharaoh's tomb. The cube was at the head of a shaft, about seven feet on a side, that fell straight down into the darkness beneath the wrecked foundation.

"The shaft is about a hundred feet deep," said King. He was scowling again. He plucked at one of the steel cables that ran down the center of the shaft. "There's an elevator car down there at the bottom of the shaft." He looked around at our puzzled faces. "A box. It rides up and down on these cables. If somebody goes down to activate the generator and bring it up, the rest of us can ride down in comfort."

"Volunteers?" asked Toby, looking around.

Lindy stepped forward. I put my hand on the cable a second before she did. For a moment, hands touching, we just looked at each other. Then Lindy tried to stare me down.

I grinned at her. "Me first."

Lindy lifted her chin. "You think you climb better than I do? Shall we have a little race and see?"

I shook my head. "There has to be something I do better than you," I reminded her. "Everybody has a specialty. You want climbing, you call a cat."

"You can't climb everything," Lindy replied. "Suppose something goes wrong. Suppose you can't get out again?"

"I promise to scream for help," I said.

Lindy released the cable. "Oh, all right."

I took a long look around at my friends. With a line of anxiety between her eyebrows, Toby was studying the open shaft. Esteban was watching Lindy, his dark eyes serene. Spike was leaning into the shaft, trying to guess the exact distance of the drop. Lindy was glaring at me. "After all," I told her, "you can't be the best at everything."

Becky pulled off her red gauntlets and handed them to me. "Here, you'll probably need these."

"Thanks." I pulled them on. The leather was still warm from her hands, which were even bigger than mine. The gloves were soft and loose but felt alive. I turned them over. The palms were stained with work. I wondered if she'd worn them at Rose Hill, and if she had, what the Lesters thought of red leather work gloves. "They're perfect." I turned to King. "How do I get out of the shaft and into the car?"

"There's a service hatch in the roof," King replied. "The

hatch handle should be easy to find, even in the dark. Once you're inside, the control panel activates the generator. You'll get lights first, then the rest of the power should kick in."

"Service hatch — right," I said, and took my place in the mouth of the shaft. The first moment was the worst, when I had a choice and could have stepped back to firm ground. I took a deep breath of chilly air and collected myself. This is part of being a River Rat, I thought. And after all, I was only doing what Jake would have done. The thought of Jake, back on board the *River Rat*, steadied me. Ankles wrapped around the cable to slow me, gloved hands strangling the cable, I started down.

The trip took a few minutes, plenty long enough for me to wish I'd never started. By the time I reached the bottom of the shaft, my ankles were sore, the palms of my hands were hot even through Becky's gloves, and I was good and scared. With the roof of the elevator car solid under me, I took a few fast breaths of stale air and let go of the cable. I pulled off Becky's gloves and stuck them in my belt. Working by touch, trying not to look up at the square of sky overhead, I found the service hatch. Once open, it was about sixteen inches on a side. I wedged myself through into the smaller dark of the car.

I fell wrong. When I got up, it took me a moment to recover my bearings. Three walls of the car were smooth metal, cold to the touch. The fourth had a vertical crack that separated the door panels, and a set of plastic squares that felt like the control panel at the top of the shaft. I found a pattern of raised dots on each square. The company that made the elevator had designed it well. Too bad I had no idea what the dots meant. At random I poked all the squares. Nothing happened.

I stood in the dark and thought about dying in an elevator car one hundred feet underground. The air in the car wasn't wonderful, but with the hatch open overhead I was in no danger of suffocation. Still, there was no way I could reach the hatch without help. I thought about screaming for help. Somebody, maybe Lindy, could slide down the cable and hand me a rope through the service hatch. That would suit Lindy. I could almost hear the smugness in her voice when I gave her a chance to rescue me. I decided not to scream and poked the squares again.

The elevator lights came on.

I looked around. The metal walls were polished like a mirror, so from all sides other Tomcats looked back at me, wild-eyed and worried. I stared at the panel of squares, wondering which had been the right one. None were marked Lights. I pressed one marked Door Open.

The metal panel slid aside. With the doors open, the air in the car was better but still pretty stale. I stepped to the threshold and leaned forward. Wakened by my touch on the squares, the generator was powering the Pharaoh's tomb for the first time in years. As I looked out of the elevator, the overhead lights flickered on one by one, running the length of a great white room lined with colored doors.

What the light revealed made me swallow hard and push the Door Close square. I touched the Up button and spent the short trip staring at my reflection in the elevator door. I no longer looked wild-eyed and worried. I looked as blue as Bud, as if I was just about ready to vomit.

When the door slid open at the top of the shaft, I kept my finger on the Door Open square. I couldn't think of anything to say. After a moment of staring at me, everyone got quiet. When they squeezed into the car with me, I pushed Door Close and Down, and we descended to the Pharaoh's tomb. No one said a word on the way.

At the bottom of the shaft, as soon as the metal panel slid open, I put my finger back on Door Open and held it there because, seeing what I had seen, no one wanted to get off. Instead we stood silent and stared at the brilliantly lit disorder before us. For, like the tombs of the true pharaohs, this vault had been stripped by looters.

10

THE
PHARAOH'S
TOMB

BARS OF LIGHT ON THE CEILING GLARED
down at the crates and cartons scattered everywhere.
Maybe there had been a method in their arrange-
ment once. Now there was none. Some boxes had been opened
and emptied. Others had been crushed beneath sliding crates
filled with still more boxes. There were heaps of trash everywhere, spilling through doors into the empty rooms that opened
off the central chamber. It was a mess. And it wasn't even a clean
mess, because it had all been there so long it had settled into tired
piles gone faintly gray with dust.

King got off the elevator first. I followed him. We picked
our way in silence past a heap of dusty orange pellets spilled out
of a box marked "Cheezos." We wandered from one opened
crate to another. The pellets crumbled when we stepped on them,
turning into orange dust with a faint, stale crunch.

As she walked through the maze of trash, Toby's face was,
for once, unreadable. She had her hands out of her pockets and
she touched things gently as she went, almost as if she were feeling her way in the dark. One by one, the rest of us gave up our

attempts to find order in the slumped boxes and came to a halt, looking around at each other in silence. Toby went on, doggedly sidling through the trash until she found the long wooden box that had once held guns.

The top of the crate was lying a few feet away, under an empty metal box enameled white with a red X on it. The only thing left in the wooden box was a trace of the grease the firearms had been packed in. Toby bent down to touch the grease and rose, rubbing her thumb across her fingertips. Her mouth relaxed, and as it did I could read her face again. There was sorrow there, and anger, and relief, or something like it. After the relief came despair.

Spike met my eyes and jerked his head a little. I joined him in one corner of the room and began a noisy, pointless search of the remaining boxes. Anything to break the silence that had suddenly filled the room.

Spike scooped an armful of foil packets from a torn carton marked Arctic-pak Foods. "Turkey tetrazzini," he read, scanning the labels. "Freeze-dried ice cream, 'like they eat in space.' Hey, do you think this stuff is food?"

Our search wasn't pointless after all. Little by little, as we worked, we began to see not what was missing, but what was still there. Water, light, food, books, tools, even a carton of flashlights and live batteries. In a broken crate of ammunition, I discovered six neglected shells.

"Hey, clothes," Spike called. "All the same color, all the same size — but clothes!"

Lindy held up a white cotton shirt and squinted critically at King. "Gee, you used to be a much cleaner guy."

King paid no attention. Touching nothing, he moved from the central room into each of the side chambers in turn. He stopped at the open door of a big room with curiously cushioned walls and spoke, without looking around to see if anyone listened. "This was my studio. I had my first Strat on a stand over there in the corner. Should have been in a museum, but I liked to have it around." He looked at the ceiling. If I hadn't seen him blink hard, I would never have guessed how upset he was.

King went on. "I had every session I played stored on digital audio. Hell of a system. My friend Woody set it up for me. I swapped him a case of fancy French champagne for his time. He wanted to break a bottle over the board to christen it, like an ocean liner. I wouldn't let him, though. Stuff cost too much to pour on the floor. Wouldn't have done the system any good either. Woody knew that. He just wanted to see me cheap out for a change." He shook his head. "Damn, I loved this place. And somebody got in here and took it all. They stripped me. My music is gone."

"You've still got it," Lindy said. "We heard it aboard the *River Rat*."

It looked to me like King smiled at her, but his mouth was twisted a little and that made it hard to be sure.

"They took it all — and left a generator?" Spike demanded. "What was wrong with those guys?"

"They must have robbed this place before the Flash," Esteban replied. "They took everything they found valuable then. And they never came back for the treasure that is truly precious. Water. Shelter. Light."

"It doesn't have the one thing we need," said Toby.

173

"We can't bargain for Jake and the *Rat* without guns," said Lindy.

"But we are spared a dilemma," said Esteban. "You won't persuade me that we could ever have traded guns to the Lesters." He eyed the empty crate that had once held rifles. "Perhaps it is as well that the temptation has been removed."

"Temptation," Toby said and her face lit up. She held out her hand to me. "The ammunition, Tomcat."

I gave her the six rifle shells. The metal in her palm gleamed dully in the bright light of the vault. "Well," she said, her voice thoughtful, "what do you know? Bargaining chips."

THAT NIGHT WE found treasure in the Pharaoh's tomb after all. Among the wreckage the robbers had left behind, we found preserved food to add to our supplies. The vault had a system that purified and stored water. While we were drinking all the water we wanted and refilling our water flasks, King introduced us to the control that heated the water. By the time Spike, Lindy, and I had tried that out, we had gotten so wet it seemed pointless not to wash. Toby and Esteban watched us patiently for a while, then went off with King to the ransacked stores and returned with fresh clothing.

"You can't just splash water on the floor like that," Becky told us, as Toby and Esteban sized the clothes against us. "Anyway, that room isn't big enough for five people. One at a time."

"Bossy," said Spike, brushing wet hair out of his eyes.

"Look, I agreed to help you, but don't push your luck," Becky said. "I left Rose Hill looking for a better place. I'd be a fool not to realize this is it. But I don't want it wrecked before I ever get to live here."

"A little water never hurt anything," Spike replied, but he followed us out and let Becky take first turn at bathing.

When Becky came out, Toby took her place. King borrowed Becky's long knife. When he was done, Becky's light brown hair lay in a wet nest on the floor. With short hair Becky should have looked more like Bud than ever, but she didn't. She looked younger, and the lines at the corners of her mouth looked more like dimples than wrinkles. Her khaki shirt was damp.

As I looked at Becky, I felt my ears start to get warm and turned my attention to King before anyone could notice and make remarks.

"What do you think?" Becky turned to King and demanded, "Will I pass for Bud?"

"At a distance," said King, "in the dark. If you don't breathe."

Becky ran her fingers through her cropped hair. "You're not much good at cutting hair," she countered. "I can do better myself."

King handed her the knife. "Prove it."

Becky took the long blade and eyed King's straggling rattail hair speculatively. "Can I?" she asked.

King shrugged. "Sure, Becky. Hack away."

Becky sliced off a hank of hair and rubbed her fingers gingerly on her jeans. "You better wash it first," she advised. "Unless you want me to just snap it off in pieces."

When Toby was done, King took her place. King stayed in the bathroom so long that steam billowed out when he finally opened the door.

"All right," he said to Becky, "do your worst." He was wearing clothes out of storage, which fit him, since they were his clothes. His tan trousers showed signs of wear earned long ago, but they were clean and unripped. His white shirt was a little loose around the collar and a little tight at the waist, but he looked good despite the hair that hung wet and tangled on his shoulders.

"What do you know, it's not mud colored," observed Becky. She took hold of a lock of his gray-streaked black hair and flourished the knife. "Hold still."

One by one, we washed off the grime of our travels. The rest of us didn't take too long, because King had finished the hot water during his turn. But for us, cold water was no novelty and clean clothing was. Even Esteban, hampered with the splint on his arm, took his turn gladly.

I was last out. Esteban had located a white shirt for me, with all its buttons and everything, which fit great except it was too wide in the shoulders and too long in the sleeves. I shook my hair nearly dry and rolled up the sleeves. There was no choice but to put my old jeans back on. I can stand a lot, but I draw the line at pulling up borrowed baggy pants every two minutes. I rinsed out my socks and twisted them good, then gathered up my jacket, dirty shirt, wet socks, and sneakers. Barefoot, I emerged from the bathroom.

King had shut down part of the vault's support system for the night so the lights were dim. The white room was deserted. I made my way among the tumbled crates and cartons, across the chilly tile floor. As I passed the door of the studio, Lindy came out. She looked mad.

"I've been waiting for you," she said, her hand on my sleeve. "Bud said some things I think we better get straight."

"All right," I replied. "But remember what a jerk he was."

"I remember," Lindy said. "He thought I . . ." She stopped and took a deep breath. "He said you . . ." She released my arm. "Forget it."

I followed Lindy into the studio. In the wedge of light from the outer room, I could see she was wearing a shirt like mine. It clung to her in a way I could not help but admire. Her pale hair was a damp mane to her shoulders, a narrow braid woven here and there in the blond tangle. Looking at her made it hard for me to think. My ears started to get hot again. I was glad of the dim light. "Are we talking about what I think we're talking about?" I asked.

"He said you told him I was a girl and you said it was okay for him to . . ." Lindy broke off to choose the perfect word and finally finished, " . . . insult me."

"I never told that guy anything. Bud guessed you're a girl," I said. "He was *such* a jerk. I figured you'd want to put him in his place yourself." I should have quit talking right there. Instead I went on, getting more confused with every word. "I thought if *I* did it, it would look like I thought what he thought. But I never thought about it that way until he talked to me . . . I think." I trailed off.

Lindy met my gaze squarely. She didn't look mad anymore. She looked kind of pleased. "Tomcat, do you like me?" she asked.

I looked squarely back at her. "Don't you know I do?" I swallowed hard. "Do you like me?"

"What do you think?" she asked.

"I don't know," I said honestly.

Lindy grinned at me. In the dim light her green eyes were alight with joy and wickedness. "Good."

WE LEFT THE Pharaoh's tomb early the next morning. First came Toby, then Esteban. I don't think they said a word to each other. I know they didn't talk to anyone else. After them came King and Becky, leading the horse loaded with wooden crates — the kind of wooden crates that guns and ammunition come in. Spike and Lindy and I walked together at a safe distance behind the horse. The clean clothes we'd gotten from King's supplies were stowed safely in our packs and we were back in the clothes we'd been wearing ever since we left the *River Rat*. It wouldn't do to confuse the Lesters.

It's a lot easier to spot a city than the foundation of a ruined house. After a safe night, with our goal in plain view, we moved fast, walking almost in step. The morning hurried along with us. By midday we were headed north along the western edge of the city, trying to skirt the tangle of railroad tracks.

"This plan is not going to work," said Spike. "Look at the way Becky walks. She doesn't look a bit like Bud."

The sun was as high as it was going to get, and Spike doesn't like the sun much. It makes him cranky. Always ready to share our opinions, no matter what the topic, Lindy and I joined in the discussion. The three of us had fallen far enough behind the others that we judged it safe to start disagreeing.

"It's a pretty good plan," said Lindy. "We don't have time for anything fancy."

"We've got nothing to worry about," I said. "I don't think the Lesters are too sharp."

"Oh, come on," exclaimed Spike. "Look at her. Nobody's that dumb."

"They didn't notice anything about Lindy or Toby," I replied. "They won't notice anything about Becky."

"Bud noticed," Lindy said darkly.

"They didn't know Lindy or Toby," Spike said. "They know Becky. And what about that horse?"

"They think King stole the horse," I replied. "Bud said so."

"It will never work," Spike said.

"The sun's getting to you, that's all," I said. "We'll let you sit in the shade when we stop to eat."

"We're not stopping," Spike said. "Toby says we're going straight through."

"Not stopping to eat?" I asked, amazed. "But we've got space ice cream."

"We've got to be back at the *Rat* before dark," Lindy said. "We need poor light to pass Becky off as Bud. We'll never do it in daylight, and if we wait for dark, they'll probably have torches. Much after dusk, or much before it, we just don't stand a chance."

By late afternoon Esteban was leading us along the river. It was hard to believe it was our own river. It seemed too narrow. I could have pitched a stone to the far shore. Only the water seemed familiar, running brown and oily between banks edged with dry reeds.

Esteban had insisted that we take a route north of the city, even though it was unfamiliar to King. By meeting the river above the rapids, and by following it down as far as the *Rat*, he hoped to avoid meeting any wild boys. I was glad he'd left our old route. This way was shorter and safer, and best of all it avoided Bud's grave. We followed the river into the corridors of the city.

It was hard to keep our course. We were drawn farther and farther from the river and soon found ourselves in a maze of streets. Esteban seemed uneasy. He urged us on with such zeal that even Toby gave him a questioning glance. Before very long I was uneasy too. There was a cold feeling on the back of my neck. It wasn't the wind either. Someone was watching me.

We hurried.

In the shadows of a street crossing, Esteban lifted his hand and pointed into the wind. I turned my head and caught, from far behind us, a faint cry. It was familiar. The sound of sea gulls.

"Sea gulls?" Spike looked offended. "Here?"

Esteban shook his head.

Short and sad, the faint cries rose and fell, approaching from a distance.

"Wild boys," said Esteban.

I cocked my head. It sounded like sea gulls to me.

"Let's get out of here," said King.

We picked our way along the wrecked street as fast as the horse would let us go. The sound of the gulls came closer, crossed behind us, divided, and followed us on either side. I could feel eyes watching me.

"They're between us and the river," said Toby. She looked grim.

The noises were all around us now.

Spike stopped to spin on his heel, searching the broken street around us as the noises came nearer. "I can't see them."

"Let's get out of here," King said again.

"Where are they?" Spike demanded.

"Let's go," said Toby. "This way." She led us into a narrow street.

"I don't think we want to wait to see them," Lindy told Spike.

"Let's go faster," added King.

"Don't panic," said Toby.

"You'll only alarm them," added Esteban.

"They alarmed me first," countered King. "They give me the creeps."

"These are wild boys, remember?" said Lindy. "If we just ignore them for about fifteen minutes, they'll get sidetracked with something else and forget all about us."

From the wrecked building to our right, someone threw a piece of glass. It hit the street in front of the horse and shattered with a pleasant chime. The horse shied. Becky and King hauled at the bridle and steadied the animal. Ears flat against its head, nostrils flared, the horse balked.

"Move it," hissed Toby.

Prodding and pushing, Becky and King got the horse to take a step forward. Another piece of glass shattered almost between the animal's forelegs. We all shied. The horse made a large circle around us, with Becky clinging to one rein and swearing.

King ducked the horse and a rock as he looked up at Lindy. "Think it's been fifteen minutes yet?"

The wild boys were sailing glass and stones out of windows on either side of the street by this time, small stones mostly, but some as big as my palm.

Becky and the horse were veering from side to side down the narrow street, as debris permitted. We pursued her. The sound of sea gulls mingled with the sound of breaking glass.

Just ahead of me Lindy jumped and clapped her right hand down hard on her left wrist. When she took her hand away, both wrist and palm were smeared with red.

"Let me look at that," King ordered.

"Keep moving," snapped Toby.

"It's nothing," Lindy snarled. "Just a scratch." She put her hand back over it. Her green sleeve oozed red as she ran. Spike and I flanked her, each putting a hand under her elbow. She didn't need our support, but she let us bracket her as we ran.

We matched strides until King shouldered Spike aside to catch Lindy's arm. "I've got to see it," he replied with a snarl matching Lindy's. "You could run yourself to death like this."

Becky and the horse widened their lead as we paused. Esteban kept after Becky. Toby paused and turned back to us.

"Just a scratch," Lindy mumbled.

"Sure, it's just a scratch," King told Lindy. He pulled her sleeve free and started to wind it clumsily around her wrist. "So what's the big idea, bleeding like this? You want to give me heart failure?"

If Lindy answered him, I didn't hear her. A chunk of cement the size of a melon shattered at King's feet, and I was running back the way we'd come.

In the empty street, with only the stones and glass to judge my audience by, I put back my head and howled. To be honest, I'd intended to copy the sea gull cry, but something in my throat was so tight that the first sound came out strangled, a yip like a coyote's. So I tried to howl like a coyote, five or six short sharp calls, then the wail, unraveling into silence. It sounded weird, but it got their attention. In fact, it sounded so different from what I'd meant to do, I almost scared myself. Before the next rock fell, I was doing my version of the wild boy dance, half step dance, half tumbling run, along the cluttered street.

I started the first line of running flips before I remembered what would happen when I put my bare hands down on broken glass. In the long moment before my hands touched the ground, I wished hard for Becky's gloves. No good wishing, though.

I cut my right hand on the first flip. Even though I saw the piece of glass that did it, I couldn't feel the cut right away. I was back on my feet, panting, at the end of the flips, before the first twinge of pain got through to me. And then I was just glad it was only the one cut. Could have been worse.

In the silent street the wild boys came toward me, picking their way across the broken glass. First among them came Red, the knotted fringe of his scarf lifting in the breeze.

I wished I could look back and see where Toby and the others were. I hoped they were running. But I didn't want to remind the wild boys of what they'd been doing before I distracted them.

Red came close, his eyes bright on mine. "Teach me that," he said.

I took a deep breath and tried hard to remember what Esteban always said about self-control. All I could think of was the frogs of sense weakness. "Practice is the best of all instructors," I said finally. I don't know what it meant, but it sounded all right. My voice was back to normal.

"Teach me," said Red. The rest of the wild boys drew into a circle around us.

I put my hand into the pocket of my jeans. It was starting to hurt some. Not much, but I didn't want to distract the wild boys with the sight of blood. You never know.

"I'll tell you how I learned," I said.

"Don't tell," said Red. "Show."

I wiped my hand as I pulled it out of my pocket, bent quickly, and did a handstand.

Red copied me, bending down and levering himself into a near handstand before he fell sideways. The others followed his example, giggling.

I held the handstand until my temples hammered. A bit clumsily, I came back down and stood beside Red. As I straightened, Red saw the blood on my hand.

"Hey!" He caught my wrist. Grinning, he ran his fingers across my palm and daubed blood in a line from cheek to cheek across the bridge of his nose. Deftly, he did the same to me. "Blood brothers!"

"Great," I said. "Blood brothers." I put my hand back in my pocket.

"Will you give me a ride on your boat, blood brother?" asked Red.

"It's not my boat," I answered.

"It's not?" Red looked surprised. "Whose boat is it?"

"It belongs to my friends," I explained.

"Some friends," said Red. "They left without you."

I turned to look. There was nothing in the street to look at. I didn't feel as glad about that as I had expected I would.

"Don't look so downhearted," said Red. He clapped me on the shoulder and told me cheerfully, "You're my blood brother — I'll get you into the wild boys."

"Great," I said. At least I'd know when the *River Rat* got away from the Lesters. They were sure to whistle when they cast off. I wondered what the wild boys would think of the *Rat*'s steam whistle. I wondered what the Lesters would think of the wild boys.

"Come on," said Red. He jerked his head back at the building behind us.

"Come on where?" I asked.

"The clubhouse," Red replied. "On the way, we'll do your initiation. That's just a custom of ours, of course."

"What initiation? Am I your blood brother or aren't I?"

"Almost," agreed Red. "Coming?"

Someone behind me said, "He's not coming."

"I'm coming," I said quickly.

But not in time to keep something from falling on my head.

A WALK IN
THE DARK

HERE WAS SOMETHING WRONG WITH me. My head hurt. I opened my eyes. It was dark. And it was cold. I was alone, lying on the cold hard ground in the dark. I put my left hand up and found my forehead, ran my fingers back — and discovered that my hair was gone. There was nothing left but a few patches of stubble. I had no hair.

For a moment I lay perfectly still. This was a dream. I would wake up. I willed myself to wake up. Then I remembered the littlest pouch on Wilson's belt, and the black hair stuffed inside. This was no dream. Shaken, I took stock of what the wild boys had done to me. Not very much, luckily. My head ached. My right hand was hurting a lot. The palm was caked with dried blood and throbbing. Could have been worse.

After a while I sat up. In addition to my hair, I was missing my blanket roll, my water flask, and my packet of food. Cross-legged in the dark, head pounding, I felt my forehead again. There was a lot more of it than I was used to. I groaned.

From overhead, metal scraped metal. I looked up as one of the wild boy lamps was lowered through a grate in the ceiling.

"Don't look so downhearted." Red's voice came from the grate. "Here's a light for you. Don't drop it."

I grabbed the cord as soon as the can of bad-smelling oil was within reach. Instantly whoever held the other end let go. Like I was going to climb up it hand over hand or something. I put the lamp down on the floor of the passage and looked back up at the grate. "What's the idea?" I demanded. "I thought we were blood brothers."

"You're all right," Red replied. "If you take the right turnings, there's enough oil in the lamp to show you the way out of the cave. When you get out, you'll be a wild boy just like us. We'll give you your hair back, too."

I snorted. "In a bag. No thanks."

"It's all part of the initiation," Red replied.

"Why do I have to be initiated?" I protested. "Why *me?*"

Red sounded like he was smiling. "We talked it over. Remember the first night we found you and your friends? You were the only one who followed our lights."

"That was a mistake," I said. "I left my post. That was wrong."

"It was the wild boy thing to do, though," said Red. He still sounded pretty pleased with things. "Now you'd better get started. The oil won't last forever. Remember, you'll get out if you take the right turnings."

"How about some water?" I demanded. "How about something to eat?"

No answer.

With my good hand I took the lamp by its cord. In its yellow light, I looked around and tried a few steps. I decided if I went slow I could walk pretty well.

The passage, which smelled like cold cement and wet dirt, was too straight to be anything natural. I remembered the tour Zeke had given me at the ramp. Cave, my eye, I thought. Caves don't have grates in the ceiling. The place had to be man-made.

Left or right? I tried to gauge which way the air current was going by the flame, but the lamp flickered without any pattern. I finally chose left because that's the way the chill on my scalp told me to go. Until my hair grew back, I figured my scalp was the most sensitive thing about me.

The ceiling in the passage was low. After about fifty yards, I saw a black mark on the rough surface overhead, where someone had held a candle or a lamp high enough to draw an arrow in lamp black. The arrow pointed back the way I'd come. The current of chill air on my scalp hadn't changed. I decided to ignore the arrow. Too obvious.

The passage branched at regular intervals, sometimes at right angles, sometimes in curves. In places the walls were patched with mold. For a while I followed a passage with rails like train tracks down the middle of the floor. It ran into a wall of cement blocks. There was an arch on either side, so I had another choice between left and right. After I thought about it for a long time, I decided on the right arch.

I saw no more arrows. Once I walked under another grating, but it was far out of reach and I had no way to climb the bare wall. I walked slowly but not steadily. Every three hundred paces, I sat down whether I needed to or not.

Never once did it occur to me to go back where I started and try again. It just never crossed my mind. It took all my attention to keep going forward.

Once I stood for a long time, listening to the sound of water running. I listened and listened and could not tell where the sound came from. It might have been running beneath the passage. When I moved, it faded after a few steps.

I walked steadily on, fighting the thought I'd changed direction somehow and was headed back the way I'd come. That was when the lamp went out.

For a moment I stood still in the perfect darkness. Thirsty, hungry, cold, and tired, I was ready to admit I was long since lost. But sitting down wouldn't do me any good. And no one else was going to get me out of the wild boys' cave. I am not the smartest River Rat. I am not the strongest, or the best-looking, or even the fastest. But I have a good claim to being the stubbornest. That's probably why it never occurred to me to go back. Instead, I thought hard about things for a minute or so. Then, carrying my useless lamp, I walked forward slowly.

After a while I realized I was humming to myself, a tuneless buzz. I paused, struggling to identify the melody that had come loose from my memory. After a few moments, it came back to me — Lindy's practice piece. I remembered the last time I'd heard it, back home aboard the *River Rat*. I wondered if I'd ever hear Lindy play again. That thought made me draw a long, shaky breath.

Lindy's marching song came back to me: *Pretty work, brave boys, pretty work, I say* . . . "*Oh, I wish I were at home,*" I sang, "*on board the* River Rat. *Say I'm going away on board the* River Rat . . ." My voice wobbled. So what? No one could hear me.

Singing made it easier to walk into the darkness. After a while my throat was so dry I was just whispering the words, but I kept on anyway. It cheered me up.

Eventually I came to a very narrow passage, where the air current drew me forward eagerly. I could smell fresh air, and the draft on my scalp made me shiver. By touch, I worked my way deeper into the fresh air until my hands met a flat wall at right angles to my passage. A dead end. I craned my neck, drew in a deep breath of the chilly air, and saw, far over my head, an open hatch filled with stars.

For a moment, the mere sight of the sky filled me with joy. Then common sense returned. I leaned against the flat, final wall of the dead end, and took stock.

I had no water. That was the worst. The hunger, the head-ache, the pain in my hand, none of that mattered beside the thirst. I let myself consider what it would be like to be stuck in the cave a long time. I was lucky to have found an open spot. If it rained, perhaps I could use the empty lamp to gather water. A little rainwater might keep me going long enough to starve to death.

With a jolt I remembered I'd eaten only that morning. I'd only been thirsty part of one day and I was already feeling sorry for myself. Disgusted, I slid down the wall into a crouch. I set the lamp aside and put my face in my hands. They shaved my head for nothing, I thought. I can't even join the wild boys.

The same part of me that had reminded me that I wasn't starving to death yet told me calmly, *Not can't — won't.* And I knew beyond any doubt that whatever else I did or didn't do, I wasn't about to join up with the wild boys.

I thought it over, sitting there in the dark. The wild boys

were all right in their way. It wasn't the neatest way. It sure wasn't the quietest way. But I was never much for neat or quiet myself. So why was I suddenly so positive that I couldn't live with them?

I studied the matter for a while. Esteban's words came back to me: *The longest way round is the shortest way home.*

The *River Rat* was my home in a way that had nothing to do with the orphanage. I belonged there. I belonged with the other Rats. And it wasn't in me to give that belonging away to another home, another family.

So what I had to do was get out of the mess I was in. Somehow. And get back to the *River Rat*. Somehow.

After all, I told myself sternly, anything a wild boy can do, a River Rat can do better. Just because I hadn't found my way out yet didn't mean I wasn't going to. In fact, I had a big advantage. Red had told me there was a way out somewhere. If a wild boy could find it, so could I. A little walking never hurt anybody.

I felt so much better, I spoke out loud. "Don't let the frogs of sense weakness kick you around," I said. With my good hand, I started to push myself to my feet.

My palm came down on something soft and damp and cold. I jerked back and wiped my hand on my jeans. As I grimaced with disgust, I smelled what I'd put my hand in, a sharp sweet scent almost like cider. My stomach growled at the thought of cider. I reached down carefully and picked up the thing I'd touched. It was an apple core, shriveled and soft. *My* apple core.

I scrambled to my feet. The stars overhead were spinning. Clumsy with impatience I groped over the walls with my good hand until I found the bottom rung of the service ladder, like a giant staple in the wall. For a moment I just stood there, pressing my hand against the cold metal, trying to hold the world still. It wouldn't do me any good to miss my grip halfway up the ladder. As soon as the stars were steady again, I let out a long, shaky breath and began to climb.

WHEN I WAS out and safe beside the hole in the uneven, cluttered street, I lay quiet for a long time, just breathing in the fact that I was free. It was a clear, cold night with a light breeze out of the west. By the angle of the Dipper, I figured it was about midnight. Unless I'd been in the wild boy caves for more than a day, it was less than twelve hours since I'd left my friends among the breaking glass. Less than six hours since they'd put the plan to work and won the *River Rat* back — or lost her.

I tried to fit the hours together. Just this time last night, I thought, Lindy was stopping me on my way from the shower. Just this morning I ate breakfast. Just this afternoon I had hair. I shivered. It all seemed like it happened a long time ago. To someone else.

From my memory of the day I'd finished that apple and thrown the core down the hole, I had my bearings. I knew where the river was. I knew where we'd moored the *River Rat*. And though the *Rat* was probably long gone, I knew that the river was where I should go. After all, the river would lead me downstream to Pig's Eye. I could work for my keep there while the winter came and went. In the spring, when the last of the ice was out, the *River Rat* would bring the mail, and I would be welcomed back on board again.

The longest way round is the shortest way home. If I'd learned anything down in the wild boys' cave, it was that I was a River Rat whether I was aboard her or not. Pig's Eye would be a long walk and a long wait, but the *River Rat* was worth it. I got to my feet.

BY THE TIME I could hear the sound of the rapids, I could smell the river. I was already walking slowly, but I slowed still more as I neared the shore. It would do me no good to trip and end up in the river. At the top of the riverbank, I stopped to stare. Even by starlight I could see the shifting white water of the rapids. There was light enough to make out the *River Rat*, still at her mooring in the calmer water downstream. I stood there blinking, trying to believe I really saw her.

So I never heard my attacker. Something hit me between the shoulder blades and I folded like a hand of cards.

My face was in the dirt and it felt like someone was sitting on me. My wrists were twisted behind my neck. Quick hands searched me. The search hit a tender spot. I made a small noise into the dirt, and when my wrists were twisted tighter, made another, not so small.

"It's Tomcat," hissed Lindy. "Let him up."

"It's a wild boy," Spike hissed back. "It's got to be. He's bald."

"I don't care if he's got quills like a porcupine, this is Tomcat."

"He smells sort of like Tomcat." Spike sounded doubtful.

I was glad of the dark, grateful for the chance to turn my face to the ground. I let myself lie still, tried to hide my relief, while they argued.

Finally Spike let my wrists go, and the weight on top of me withdrew. "You okay, Tomcat?" Spike whispered.

I couldn't think of anything to say to that, so I just whispered yes.

"Tomcat?" Lindy sounded worried. Gentle hands turned me over so I could see the stars again. "Are you okay?"

"Yes," I said again. This time they heard me. "Got any water?" I asked.

Lindy helped me lift my head, and Spike held his flask for me. Maybe I left him some water in the bottom. I sure tried to.

"What happened to you?" Spike asked, when I had made myself quit drinking.

"Wild boys wanted me to join up," I explained. I closed my eyes. The water was sweet in my belly. My friends hadn't left me. Spike was blocking most of the breeze. Best of all, my head was cradled in Lindy's lap, and Lindy's hand lay warm across my forehead. I didn't want to move again, ever.

IT OCCURRED TO me that somebody was whispering. After I thought about it, it occurred to me that somebody was whispering about me. Rude. It occurred to me that my eyes were shut. Maybe somebody thought I was asleep. I opened my eyes. There was a small blossom of yellow light, close enough to make the shadows dance. I flinched back into a corner of masonry.

"Steady there, Tomcat," said King. His hand on my shoulder was gentle. "You're doing fine. How does your head feel?"

I realized he was holding one of the flashlights from the Pharaoh's tomb. Even with his fingers shielding it, there was light enough for him to take a good look at me. We were out of the night breeze in the shelter of a ruined wall. Someone had tucked me into a blanket so tightly I had to struggle to move my arms. Beyond the glow of King's light, the stars had moved on without me. "Fine," I said.

"Good," said King. He turned the light so it dazzled me. When I tried to turn away, he held my chin. "I like a patient who believes me. You know who you are and how many fingers you've got on each hand, don't you?" He kept the light in my eyes.

I realized he was waiting for an answer. "I think so," I replied. I managed to untuck the blanket.

King let go of my chin.

I looked at my hands. The right one was bandaged, not very neatly. The bandage smelled like the supplies from the Pharaoh's tomb. My hand still hurt.

"No fair peeking," said King. "Any other rips or dents you think I should know about? Spine? Ribs?"

"I'm fine," I said. I pulled the blanket back up to my chin. "What's going on, anyway?"

"Nothing at the moment," King replied. He put out the light. "Just as soon as we see some evidence that the sun ever intends to rise again, we take our places and carry on with our original plan."

"Sunset," I said. I blinked up at the stars. "The plan was for sunset."

"Well, sunset came and went, but we didn't," King replied. "Your performance gave us a chance to get away. I, for one, salute you. But your friends didn't seem to think much of your heroic gesture. First they argued until after dark about how long to wait for you. Then everyone wanted to go rescue you. Some wanted to find you and kill you and then rescue you. The others wanted to find you and rescue you and then kill you. When Spike and

Lindy brought you here, I thought the first motion must have carried."

"I heard somebody whispering," I said. "Who was here before?"

"Esteban came to see if you're ready to travel yet. I took a flyer and told him you would be soon. You are okay, aren't you?" King asked.

"Sure, I'm fine," I said. "Except for my hair."

"To be honest," King said, and for the first time his voice was serious, "you scared us all half to death. Lindy thought you were coming down with neotyphus. I don't see any sign of it, but if you do, will you please mention it?"

I'm not used to a lot of concern. From King, it took me by surprise. "You'll be the first to know," I replied.

"And another thing," King went on, "just in case no one else thinks of telling you — thanks for pulling that stunt. You probably saved our lives."

"Oh, I don't know," I said. I was grateful again for the darkness. I felt embarrassed.

"All *I* know is, those wild kids absolutely give me the creeps. And another thing — " King cleared his throat. Even he was starting to sound embarrassed. "If this works, we're all going to have to move mighty fast. Becky and I won't be able to stick around. So this might be my last chance to say it . . . I just want to thank you guys. You'll tell Toby and the others for me, won't you, Tomcat?"

"Well, okay." Toby and the others didn't need me to tell them anything. But he didn't seem to understand that. And he *had* quit calling me kid. "I'll tell them. How's Lindy's wrist?"

"Just a superficial cut," King answered. His voice was back to its normal lightness. The tone did as much to reassure me as the words. "It bled quite a lot at the time, but she seems to have forgotten all about it."

"Is everybody else okay?" I asked. "How's Esteban's arm?"

"Esteban's arm is still broken. Everyone else is fine, except Toby, who is rapidly fretting herself to the point of insanity," King replied. "But after all, insanity is nothing new to your bunch."

"She'll be better when we get the *River Rat* back," I said. "We'll all be a lot better then."

"The *River Rat* and Jake," said King.

"Well, of course, Jake," I said, and closed my eyes again.

WHEN I WOKE up, Esteban was bending over me, silhouetted against a night sky that betrayed the first symptoms of morning.

"Show time," Esteban whispered. "We're on our way back to the *River Rat*. How do you feel?"

"I wish you guys would quit asking me that," I replied, pushing my blanket aside.

"He's fine," Esteban said over his shoulder.

Behind him Toby said softly, "I'll yell at you later, Tomcat."

"I know," I said and concentrated on rolling up the blanket by touch. When I finished I joined my friends and Becky's horse. "Where's Lindy?"

"On duty," Becky replied. "She and Spike are our sentinels."

"We'll collect them on the way to the river," said Esteban.

Chirp by chirp, the birds were starting up. It was still too dark to do more than guess at shapes, but soon the light would start to rise fast. I fell in step with Esteban as we set off after Toby. King and Becky kept the horse well back at the rear. I was glad about that.

Halfway to the river, Lindy and Spike loomed up out of the darkness. There was a wild boy between them.

"Friend of yours to see you, Tomcat," Spike said. "He says he has to talk to you."

Lindy was almost on tiptoe, trying to look every way at once. "He's alone. At least, he says he's alone," she said.

I came closer and saw it was Red. There was light enough to show me the dark smudge across the bridge of his nose. My blood.

"Don't look so downhearted," I said.

Red grinned. "You found a new way out of the cave," he said. "I knew you were really a wild boy."

"Not me. Anyway, I didn't make it before the light went out."

Red shrugged. "You're still a wild boy. Here." He held out a small bag tied with cord.

When I took it I didn't have to untie the cord. The bag's lightness and softness told me what it held. "Gee," I said. "Uh, gee."

"You wear it on your belt," Red said. "Then if you have to, you can prove you're a wild boy. When your hair grows back, don't cut it. People can tell just by looking at you how long you've been a wild boy."

"Thanks, Red," I said. "Look, since we're blood brothers and all, I'd better warn you. Watch out for the Lesters. They're not very good company, if you know what I mean."

"Not good dancers?" asked Red.

"Worse than that. They are rotten in every way," I replied.

"They've been downright mean to us. If you run across one, you be careful."

"Okay," said Red. "Are you going back to your boat now?"

"Going to try," I said.

"Can I come, too?" Red asked.

"No," I said. "You probably wouldn't like it anyway. Boats are a lot of work."

"Oh," said Red. "Hey, look at this." He shrugged away from Lindy and Spike and dropped into a perfect handstand.

"Not bad," I said.

Effortlessly, Red came back to his feet. "Practice is the best of all instructors," he said. He grinned at me and swept a bow to my friends. Then, before I could say another word, he stepped back and disappeared into the waning night.

12

CHARADES

WORDLESSLY WE MADE OUR WAY TO the river. Except for the remains of my headache, I felt fine. Toby had loaned me her top hat to help conceal my baldness, so my head wasn't even cold. I felt practically chipper. But I never lost the uneasy sense that we were being watched. From their silence, I think my companions felt the same.

We were all aware that with every step we took, the eastern sky grew brighter. There was light enough already to guess at colors, and the birds were singing in earnest. Toby led us at a pace that made the horse jog to keep up. When we got close to the rapids, we slowed. The steady rush of falling water drowned most of the noise we made, but as a result we couldn't hear very well. We moved with care to the south side of the last slope before the *River Rat*'s mooring.

Toby lifted her hand and we stopped. Lindy and I were beside her, Spike just behind us. Esteban and Becky were at the horse's head, and King stood safely to one side. Turning to face us, Toby spoke, her voice strained and tired and soft, as if she had a sore throat. We all drew closer to hear her better. "We won't get another chance like this," she said.

We looked at each other. The horse lowered its head to sniff at a weed. King and Becky looked at each other over the horse's neck. Everyone looked serious.

"Make it count," said Toby.

We all nodded, even King.

Esteban stayed with King and Becky and the horse. Spike, Lindy, and I followed Toby up the broken slope and peered cautiously over the ridge of shattered concrete. High in the northeast I saw clouds, but they were the thin, patchy kind, rippled like the skin on boiled milk. It was probably going to be a nice day. Before us lay the river, the white water of the rapids to our left, the smooth dark current of the open channel to our right. Directly below us was the *River Rat*.

Toby turned back to look over her shoulder. At her signal, Esteban, King, and Becky, with the horse in tow, started up after us.

Tied at the mooring where we had left her, the *River Rat* rested quietly in the calm water. In the early light, compared with the ruins of the city, she seemed very clean. Faint gray wisps of smoke drifted from the crown of her stacks.

"Places, everybody," Lindy said out of the corner of her mouth. "Keep a sharp eye out for your cues, Tomcat. It's show time."

"Good old Jake," said Spike. "He's stoked her for us."

"I don't see any sentries," said Toby. "What a bunch of slobs." She got to her feet at the crest of the slope, fists rammed hard into her pockets. As we scrambled to our feet behind her, she started down, broken concrete skittering before her. We were

202

at the mooring before the first Lester popped out of the pilot-house door shouting an alarm.

Toby shook her head in wordless disgust.

The four of us waited at the water's edge while Lesters appeared along the rail of the main deck. One by one they came out to stare across at us and nudge each other. They didn't look any better than I remembered. When there were seven along the rail, and still no sign of Lester or Jake, Toby shouted. "Hey, Jake! Permission to come aboard."

The Lesters laughed so hard they had to lean against each other.

Toby ignored them. "Hey, Jake!" Her voice nearly cracked. She stopped shouting and waited in silence.

The Lesters took turns calling suggestions to us.

I stood between Lindy and Spike and felt my temper rise like a kettle coming to a boil. A few good remarks occurred to me, but Toby's calm sternness kept me quiet.

Above us on the crest of the slope at our backs, Esteban appeared, elbow to elbow with King. Behind them stood Becky and the horse.

One of the Lesters found the strength to push himself upright and release the deck rail. He retreated and disappeared within the *Rat*. In a few moments he was back, Lester with him, on the upper deck.

Lester leaned against the rail with both hands and took a long look at us before he spoke. "So you came back. I didn't think you would." His booming voice carried across to us easily.

"Where's Jake?" demanded Toby.

"Don't you want to talk to me?"

"No." Toby made the single word a masterpiece of disgust. "Where is Jake?"

"Your friend is busy right now." Lester scratched his stomach. "Where are my guns?"

Toby jerked her thumb over her shoulder. Esteban lifted his hand in a casual salute to indicate the crates tied to the horse.

Lester's beefy face split into a grin. "Bud, you been behaving yourself?"

It wasn't full daylight yet, but the light was getting better all the time. I couldn't see much of Becky because of the horse, but what I could see looked exactly like Becky to me, not a bit like Bud. I didn't think she stood much chance of fooling her own uncle. But people see what they expect to see. And what choice did we have? We had to try.

Becky lifted one ungloved hand in a thumbs-up gesture. King took a step back and blocked Becky from view behind the horse. I held my breath.

Lester chuckled. "You even got that horse back. That will come in handy. We're low on supplies here. I could use a square meal."

I let my breath go. At my side Lindy stiffened with indignation at the thought of eating a horse.

"Where's Jake?" repeated Toby.

"Keep your shirt on," Lester replied. "Bud, get down here. I want to see the guns."

Toby held up her hand.

Esteban took the reins away from Becky and held the horse at the top of the slope. The horse tried for a bite of Esteban. As he struggled with the animal, Becky edged farther out of Lester's line of sight. King stepped in front of her and pretended to try to help Esteban with the horse. Esteban ignored him and took a cautious step down the slope. The horse followed at the full length of its reins, ears flat with annoyance. Slowly and awkwardly, hampered by having only one hand, Esteban led it after him. He picked his way exactly halfway down the slope and stopped.

"Maybe you didn't hear me," said Toby. "Where's Jake?"

"Get him," Lester called, and left the rail to start down the steps. By the time he reached the main deck, a pair of Lesters had emerged from the engine room with Jake between them.

Jake was in his shirtsleeves, his face flushed with anger, his hair on end. There were dark smudges beneath his eyes, and he didn't look as if he'd slept or washed or eaten since we left. Except for that, he seemed all right. Even with a Lester holding each arm, he stood straight and square. His head was high and his neck was stiff.

"You okay?" Toby called. She didn't sound tired anymore.

Jake nodded. He flicked a glance from Toby to Lindy, Spike, and me, then swept a quick look up the slope to take in Esteban and the others. He looked back at Toby and nodded again. His mouth was a straight hard line.

"Now," Lester said, "get the guns the rest of the way down here."

"You keep your own shirt on," said Toby. "I'm not trading anything for anybody until I've had a chance to inspect the *River Rat*. And Jake. Let us aboard."

"You're not getting on until those guns are down here."

"How are we supposed to get them to you? Throw 'em? Put

the landing stage over and let us aboard," she said evenly, "or we take the guns back into the city and you can come and get them yourself." Toby lifted her hand again.

Before Esteban responded, Lester signaled and two of his boys came forward to struggle with the landing stage. It took them a while to get it over. I would have enjoyed watching them mess up the job a lot more if the sun had been setting instead of rising.

Toby put her fists back in her pockets. "Permission to come aboard?" she asked. Jake nodded. Toby led Lindy, Spike, and me across the landing stage. Lindy stumbled twice on the way and rubbed her forehead theatrically. As I followed I pulled Toby's hat down to my eyebrows. If I let it fall into the river, Toby would kill me.

Esteban brought the horse down the slope as far as the mooring. The horse didn't want to come with him, so it was slow going. King was still standing at the crest of the hill, Becky mostly hidden behind him.

As I stepped onto the main deck and felt the familiar lift of the river through the planks, I looked back to the mooring. The horse sniffed at the mooring line and made a disgusted noise. It shook its head. Esteban held the reins tightly. I wondered how the deck of the *River Rat* felt to him. I looked away and took my place at Toby's heels, between Spike and Lindy. The other Lesters joined us on the main deck. After a visit with the wild boys, it didn't seem like very many people at all.

Toby walked up to Lester and studied him, as if he was a new kind of lizard or bug. "Well?"

Lester jerked his chin up. At the signal, his boys released Jake and stepped back. Toby turned swiftly from Lester to Jake.

For a moment she faced him in silence. Then Toby asked again, very softly, "You okay?" and reached out to take a handful of Jake's shirt, as if to inspect the cloth. That seemed enough to assure her that he was real, that neither of them was dreaming. "Told you we'd get back," she added, her voice more normal. She let him go.

Jake's mouth tightened at the corners. It wasn't exactly a smile, but he was trying for one. "Yeah," he said. He sounded as though he hadn't spoken since we'd gone away. "We're really going through with this?"

Toby frowned. "What choice is there?"

Jake shook his head and looked past Toby to Spike. "I raked out your grates for you." He glanced at Lindy and me and added, "They ate all the oatmeal."

"Good," said Lindy.

"The guns," said Lester.

Toby turned to Lester as she jammed her fists back in her pockets. "Get all your boys out here on deck. Time for inspection."

"I inspect the guns," said Lester, "then you inspect your boat."

"Inspect this, Lester," Toby said. She brought one hand out of her pocket. On her palm gleamed six rifle shells. As Lester's eyes brightened, she dropped them on the deck. "Spike, Tomcat, start with the engine room."

"Boys, get those crates aboard," ordered Lester. "Now!"

Toby gave us a small nod. Spike and I ran for the engine room. As we went, Lindy leaned heavily against the deck rail, rubbing her forehead again.

Two of the Lesters were on the landing stage when Esteban let the reins go. The horse nipped him on the shoulder and turned. It headed back up the broken slope. Esteban shouted. The horse went faster, the boxes jolting crazily against their lashings. The pair of Lesters passed Esteban and scrambled after the horse, yelling as they went. Along the crest of the slope, King and Becky made a bad job of trying to head off the beast. When it dropped out of sight on the other side, they followed.

At the engine room Spike tossed me the shovel and jumped to his gauges. He moved from one glassed-in needle to the next, happy with what he found. "Not bad, not bad at all. Give it a couple more shovels for luck."

I scraped coal into the firebox while Spike threw a lever and two switches. He ran his hands through his hair once while he watched a needle crawl up its dial, then put both hands on the main switch. "Okay, here we go. It's show time."

"Good luck," I said. I dropped the shovel and ran.

Back out on the main deck six Lesters were staring at Lindy, who was slumped on the planks, making nasty gagging noises. Beside her, holding her head, knelt Jake. The moment she saw me coming, Toby took her hand from Lindy's face and straightened to glare at Lester.

"This kid has a bad fever," she snapped at Lester. "This is what happens when you try to deal with the wild boys. Look, I don't have time to bargain with you. The kid needs help."

"Then what are you looking at me for? What am I supposed to do about it? Get those boxes back here."

Lindy groaned.

"Fever?" asked Daryl. He took a step back from Lindy and traded nervous glances with Chuck.

The other Lesters were running up the riverbank in pursuit

of the horse. Esteban was only halfway up the slope, hand pressed against his ribs as if to get his breath.

"I'll catch that horse for you, Pa," Daryl told Lester. He sounded nervous.

"I'll help," Chuck added.

Esteban gave up his lame pursuit and came back down the riverbank. Chuck and Daryl passed him as he reached the mooring.

Lindy lay on the deck, her head in Jake's arms. She looked terrible. Her mouth hung open. Her eyes were half shut. The retching noises she made had changed to a strangled panting. Lester took a step away from Lindy as her retching started again.

"Bud!" he roared, "get that horse back here — *now*."

The horse was gone. The Lester boys followed, shouting.

The great stern wheel of the *River Rat* jerked. With a hiss of steam, a froth of creaming water, the *River Rat* came back to life.

Lester's head snapped around. At the sight of the boiling river astern, he opened his mouth to yell. "Boys! Get back here!"

The *River Rat* strained at her mooring.

Esteban reached the landing stage. At the crest of the slope, a few Lesters paused, looked back, and started to scramble down to the river.

"Go," Toby said, and ran for the pilothouse.

Lindy quit groaning and opened her eyes wide. Jake put his hands under Lindy's arms. He lifted her to her feet in one easy motion. Lindy grinned wickedly and came on guard as Lester turned toward her. "Show time," she said happily.

Esteban came silently aboard. The strain of the *River Rat*'s engines in full reverse had drawn the mooring line as tight as a guitar string. I could have danced on it sooner than cast it off. While I struggled with the landing stage, Esteban drew Becky's long knife from his belt and moved to the line. With a single slash of the blade, he cut us free.

The *Rat* jerked away from the shore and the current caught her.

Esteban and I blundered into each other. I grabbed at the rail with one hand and Toby's top hat with the other. Esteban recovered his balance without grabbing anything and glanced around. The *River Rat* jerked again, caught in the narrow channel of the river, clawing for room to turn. Esteban gazed in horror toward the pilothouse. "What is she doing to my *River Rat?*" he cried, and hurried for the steps.

I looked back at the others. Lindy had Lester squared off on the main deck. She circled him like a dancing wild boy, slid past his guard, and landed a blow on the side of his head. With a ham-colored hand, Lester swatted her away. Lindy fell back against the rail and reached to catch herself with both hands. Her injured wrist gave way beneath her. As she fell to one side, Lester swung a boot at her head. Jake lunged in to knock the burly man off balance. Lester went down and pulled Jake with him.

Esteban blew the *Rat*'s whistle, two short shrieks of farewell, and brought us about. Then we were pounding down the narrow channel of the river at a steady seven miles an hour.

It was two against one, but neither of the two was in very good shape. I wasn't either, but I started toward the fight anyway. Halfway there I remembered the top hat. There was nowhere safe to put it on deck. I hesitated for a moment, then ducked into the engine room.

"Hey, Spike," I said, "your turn to wear it for a while." I

tossed the top hat at him and spun back to the fight without waiting for his answer.

Before I joined them, Jake and Lindy had flanked Lester and pinned him on the rail. As he struggled they took a leg apiece and lifted him. For a moment he seemed to defy gravity, then he fell into the emptiness overboard. A moment of free fall, then he hit the water headfirst and went down without a bubble. Lindy gave Jake a little shove of congratulations and they both slumped against the rail, panting.

On the riverbank, the more stubborn Lesters had cornered the horse and brought it back into sight. When they saw the *River Rat* in midstream, they stopped and stared at us. As Jake, Lindy, and I watched from the deck rail, Daryl and Chuck pulled the crates free of the ropes that lashed them to the saddle. One hit the ground on a corner, split open, and spilled dirt down the broken slope. The Lesters looked at the mess for a long moment. As they stared, the horse bit its captor and broke free. With a kick for good measure, it left the Lesters behind and galloped back over the crest of the slope.

The sun was just starting to burn its way up into the sky. I could see its rim, thin as a fingernail, at the horizon. It was going to be a good day.

Jake sighed and propped himself more comfortably on the deck rail. "No guns for the Lesters," he said happily.

"No guns for anyone," Lindy said. "Bud's dead, but we didn't kill him. That's Becky with King. The wild boys gave Tomcat a haircut."

"They sure did," said Jake. He gave me a long look, plenty long enough to laugh at me if he was going to, but he wasn't going to. That's what I like about Jake.

"They made me join up," I said. "I'm a wild boy now."

"You can't be," Jake replied. "Once a Rat, always a Rat."

Before the first curve of the channel, we caught sight of the horse. The beast stood calmly while Becky pulled King into the saddle behind her. There were Lesters coming up fast, their faces beet red. But even riding double, King and Becky could outrun hunters on foot.

Esteban blew the *Rat*'s whistle again. Becky lifted a hand to wave to us. King hung on to Becky; but though he didn't wave, he watched us go past. He was too far away for me to be sure, but I think he was smiling.

Then the river took us around a bend and cut off our view. As we passed the great storage cylinders ranked along the river, Toby came down from the upper deck. Jake and I made room for her between us.

Toby looked at me, eyes narrowed. "Tomcat. What did you do with my hat?"

Without waiting to think of an answer, I ducked back into the engine room. "Spike!"

Startled, he looked up from his gauges. The hat brim tipped down over his eyes. Impatiently, he pushed it back. "What's the matter? What went wrong?"

"Nothing. Only Toby wants her hat back."

Spike took it off hastily and handed it over. "Everything else okay?"

I grinned at him. "Yeah. King and Becky got away. The Lesters are on their own. Maybe they'll find their way back to Pig's Eye."

"Or maybe they'll get the pestilence instead." Spike grinned at me, then turned to his gauges again.

Back at the rail, Toby was saying, "No Lesters — I inspect-ed." She took the top hat from me, examined it, put it on so it tilted a little bit over her left eye, and nodded to me.

"Nobody aboard but us River Rats?" asked Lindy. "No wild boys? No passengers at all?"

"Passengers are bad luck," I said. I leaned against the rail beside her.

"Lesters are bad luck, anyway," agreed Lindy.

"What about King?" asked Jake. "Does he deserve to be left here with them?"

"We only left him with one," Lindy answered, "and he didn't seem to mind her much."

"They caught that horse," Toby said. "Esteban and I saw them from the pilothouse."

"We saw, too," I said.

"I think they plan to move into his tomb together," said Lindy. "It's not a bad place, if you don't mind no windows."

"I wonder what the wild boys will make of the Lesters," I said. "Lunch, maybe?"

"Promise you'll explain all this to me," said Jake, "and I'll tell you how Lesters like to eat their oatmeal."

"We'll explain it, sure," Lindy said. She pushed her hair back from her eyes. "Spike and I saved you some space ice cream."

"Thanks," said Jake. "That sounds horrible."

Lindy shot me a look.

"It's . . . better than oatmeal," I said feebly.

"Talk later," Toby said firmly. "Move it, Tomcat. I want soundings. Give him a hand, Lindy."

With a sigh I followed Lindy forward and looked for the

sounding pole. The Lesters had made quite a mess of the deck while we were gone. Lindy found the pole under a tangle of cable, and I took my station at the rail. The greasy river water ran smooth beneath our bow. I watched the early sunlight slide on the water for a moment, listened to the steady rhythm of the stern wheel beating us along.

Ahead lay Pig's Eye landing and after that the main channel. Beyond that ran thirteen hundred miles of river, hardly a yard of it without some hazard for the *River Rat* and us. But at least on the river you can see where you're going.

I leaned out over the rail and plunged the sounding pole home. "By the mark two," I called back over my shoulder.

Behind me Lindy relayed the call, her voice clear and strong. The sun was well up now. The deck felt alive under my feet. The pole was light in my hands. In a little while, my hand would start to hurt again. I didn't care. "Mark twain!" I called.